THE FACILITATOR

IMRAN DOKADIA

INDIA • SINGAPORE • MALAYSIA

ISBN 979-8-89556-966-5

Dedicated to

My greatest treasures –

Dua, Firdaus and Mariyah.

You facilitate joy and happiness in my life.

And

To my sister

Nishat Merchant

A steadfast pillar of support and an unwavering source of love.

I wish I had the eloquence to fully express my deep gratitude and boundless love for your constant presence and unending support.

And

To

The Mrs. – My better half

Thank you for your love, patience and being who you are.

Facilitator

noun

a person or thing that makes an action or process easy or easier.

Contents

Prologue *9*

Part 1

Chapter 1 15
Chapter 2 24
Chapter 3 28
Chapter 4 32
Chapter 5 35
Chapter 6 38
Chapter 7 44
Chapter 8 53
Chapter 9 56
Chapter 10 62
Chapter 11 67

Part 2

Chapter 12 71
Chapter 13 74
Chapter 14 77
Chapter 15 80
Chapter 16 90
Chapter 17 98
Chapter 18 103

Chapter 19 105
Chapter 20 110
Chapter 21 113
Chapter 22 116
Chapter 23 119
Chapter 24 125
Chapter 25 130
Chapter 26 135
Chapter 27 140
Chapter 28 159
Chapter 29 163
Chapter 30 165
Chapter 31 172
Chapter 32 178
Chapter 33 186
Chapter 34 191
Chapter 35 195
Chapter 36 197
Chapter 37 208
Chapter 38 220
Chapter 39 227

Epilogue 231

Prologue

Shadows in the Alley

The city of Sultanabad was beginning to quiet down as the vibrant streets transitioned from the bustling chaos of the day to the subdued hum of the evening. Ihfaaz, one of India's most notorious Hawala operators, had just finished another long day of clandestine meetings and intricate transactions. He was a man of precision and routine, traits that had kept him at the top of his shadowy profession for years.

As he exited the nondescript office complex where he conducted his business, Ihfaaz took a moment to breathe in the cool night air. He pulled out a cigarette, lighting it with practiced ease, and took a deep drag. He should cut down on smoking, he thought to himself, but tonight was not the night to start. His apartment was only a short walk away, a modest place tucked away in a quieter part of the city. He preferred it that way, a semblance of normalcy amidst his chaotic and dangerous life.

The office complex was a maze of dimly lit corridors and concrete walls, a perfect facade for his operations. Ihfaaz navigated the labyrinthine passages with ease, his footsteps echoing in the silence. He pushed open the heavy door leading to the street, the hinges creaking slightly. Outside, the streetlights cast long shadows on the pavement, and the distant sounds of the city provided a constant, reassuring hum.

He walked briskly, his senses always alert, though tonight felt no different from any other. The alleyway that cut through to his apartment complex was narrow and dark, lined with dumpsters and the occasional stray cat. Ihfaaz had taken this route countless times, its familiarity lulling him into a false sense of security.

But tonight, something was different. Three men stood at the far end of the alley; their faces partially hidden by the darkness. Ihfaaz's instincts screamed at him, but before he could react, they moved with deadly precision. The men blocked the entire alley, guns drawn, and without a word, they opened fire.

Bullets sprayed wildly, ricocheting off the brick walls and the ground. Ihfaaz moved quickly, adrenaline surging through his veins. He darted to the side, using a dumpster for cover. The alley was filled with the deafening roar of gunfire and the acrid smell of gunpowder. Ihfaaz felt a searing pain as a bullet grazed his shoulder, followed by another that embedded itself in his thigh. He bit back a cry of pain, his mind racing for a way out.

The attack lasted less than two minutes, though it felt like an eternity. The contract killers, confident in their work, ceased fire and quickly retreated, leaving Ihfaaz bleeding and gasping for breath. They moved with military efficiency, disappearing into the night. Ihfaaz, his vision blurring, managed to drag himself to a nearby doorway, where he slumped down, clutching his wounds.

Upstairs in the office, the sound of gunfire had not gone unnoticed. Ihfaaz's chief assistant, Nadia, was the first to react. She had always been protective of Ihfaaz, and tonight was no different. She rushed down the stairs, followed by a few other staff members, her heart pounding in her chest.

When she reached the alley, she saw Ihfaaz slumped against the wall, blood seeping from his wounds. Panic threatened to overwhelm her, but she forced herself to stay calm. "Call an ambulance!" she shouted to one of the staff members. Then, she knelt beside Ihfaaz, her hands trembling as she checked his pulse.

Nadia knew that calling a regular hospital would attract unwanted attention. Instead, she dialled a number she had hoped she would never need to use. The hospital in which Ihfaaz was a shadow investor, discreet and efficient, was well-prepared for situations like this.

"Hello, this is Nadia," she said urgently. "We need an emergency team at our location immediately. Ihfaaz has been shot. Prepare the operating room and have Dr. Sharma on standby."

The voice on the other end responded swiftly, "Understood. We'll be there in five minutes."

Nadia hung up and turned back to Ihfaaz, her eyes filling with tears. "Hold on, Ihfaaz. Help is on the way," she whispered, gently brushing his hair away from his face. She could see the pain in his eyes, but also a flicker of gratitude.

The sound of approaching sirens filled the air as Nadia and the other staff members did their best to keep Ihfaaz stable. Within minutes, a discreet, unmarked ambulance arrived, and a team of medics rushed out, expertly assessing the situation.

As Ihfaaz was carefully loaded onto a stretcher, Nadia held his hand, not wanting to let go. "You're going to be okay," she said, more to reassure herself than him.

Ihfaaz managed a weak smile. "Thank you, Nadia," he whispered, his voice barely audible.

As the ambulance sped away, Nadia stood in the alley, her mind racing with questions. Who had tried to kill Ihfaaz? And more importantly, why? She knew she had to find answers, not just for Ihfaaz, but for herself as well.

A few blocks away, the three assassins reached their getaway car and switched to a second vehicle, a nondescript sedan parked in a deserted lot. They drove in silence, the adrenaline still pumping through their veins. As they left the city limits, a cell phone's ring broke the silence. The phone was in the glove box, an unexpected intrusion. The driver reached over, answered it, and immediately realized their mistake.

The explosion was instantaneous, a fiery blast that lit up the night sky. The car was engulfed in flames, leaving no trace of the men who had carried out the hit.

Part 1

Chapter 1

Kushalgram 15 Years Ago

Nestled in the fertile plains of eastern India, Kushalgram lay strategically near the borders of both Nepal and Bangladesh. This small town, with its bustling markets and quaint streets, was a hub of local activity and tradition. Its proximity to the international borders made it a significant player in the smuggling of high-duty items, such as gold, which flowed through the town due to its advantageous location.

Ahsan Faraz Khan was deeply entrenched in the town's dynamics. His father, Faraz Khan, a respected Pathan by lineage, had settled in Kushalgram years ago. Faraz Khan had earned immense respect in the town for his integrity and adherence to business ethics. Despite being involved in the transportation of smuggled goods, his operations were above board compared to others in the trade. Faraz Khan's uprightness and commitment to his business had earned him a respected status among both the citizens and the authorities of Kushalgram.

In contrast, Syed Fazil Hussain, the head of a rival family, had a more controversial reputation. Hussain's family was involved in similar smuggling activities but was known for taking shortcuts and engaging in morally ambiguous practices to enhance their profits. This difference in business ethics had fuelled a long-standing rivalry between the two families. Faraz Khan's adherence to principles had earned his family immense respect, while Hussain's methods often invited suspicion and distrust.

The rivalry was not just a matter of business but had seeped into the personal lives of the families, affecting social interactions and relationships within the town. Festivities and gatherings were often overshadowed by the tension between the two families, making any cross-family connections fraught with complications.

Amidst the simmering rivalry, Ahsan's family was deeply engrossed in the preparations for his elder sister's wedding. The family home was a hive of activity, with colourful lights and vibrant decorations transforming the courtyard, and the aroma of traditional sweets permeating the air. Every corner of the house was busy with relatives and workers, each contributing to the elaborate arrangements. Despite the festive bustle and the joy of the occasion, Ahsan Faraz Khan felt a profound sense of unease. The contrast between the celebration in his home and his inner turmoil highlighted the depth of his conflict.

At 22, Ahsan was in his final year of studies in computer software engineering, but he had returned to Kushalgram for his sister's wedding. According to his family's tradition, the ideal marriageable age was between 20 and 23 years. This custom placed significant pressure on young men in the community to settle down within this age range. Although Ahsan was pursuing his studies and had intentions of continuing with a master's degree, his family was insistent on having him at least get engaged before he completed his education. They believed that finding a suitable girl and securing an engagement would adhere to their cultural norms while allowing Ahsan to finish his academic commitments without delaying the marriage further.

The pressure was mounting, and Ahsan felt the weight of expectation bearing down on him. Yet, his heart was heavy with a secret that he could no longer keep hidden. His emotions were entangled in his feelings for Varda, the daughter of Syed Fazil Hussain, a girl he had admired from afar during their college days. Despite their shared experiences at college, he never mustered the courage to approach her, and his feelings remained a one-sided affair. He often found himself reminiscing about fleeting moments with her—shared smiles, accidental brushings of hands, and the occasional conversations that left him yearning for more.

The evening after his arrival, Ahsan found himself in his childhood room, staring out of the window at the wedding preparations below. The cheerful noise and bustling activity seemed like a cruel irony to his internal turmoil. Unable to bear the weight of his emotions any longer, he decided to confront the issue head-on. The room, filled with the familiar scent of old books and childhood memories, felt confining as he struggled with his decision.

After dinner, as his mother was busy organizing wedding details, Ahsan approached her, his heart pounding. "Ammi," he began softly, trying to steady his voice, "can we talk in private?"

His mother looked up from the stack of wedding invitations she was sorting through, sensing the gravity in his tone. "Of course, beta. What's troubling you?"

Ahsan led her to a quieter part of the house, a small garden area where they could speak privately. The garden was illuminated by the soft glow of lanterns, casting a warm light over the lush greenery. "Ammi," he started, his voice trembling, "I know you and Baba are looking for a match for me, and I respect that tradition. But there's something I need to tell you. I have deep feelings for someone else. Her name is Varda, the daughter of Syed Fazil Hussain. We studied in the same college, and my feelings for her have only grown stronger over the years."

His mother's eyes widened in shock. "Varda? But... our families are rivals. Your Baba and Fazil Hussain don't see eye to eye. How could you...?" Her voice trailed off, unable to fully grasp the magnitude of Ahsan's revelation.

"I know it's complicated," Ahsan said, his gaze earnest. "But I couldn't keep this from you any longer. I can't bear the thought of being engaged to someone else while my heart belongs to her."

His mother's expression softened with a mixture of concern and sadness. "This is not going to be easy, Ahsan. Our family's honour and traditions are deeply intertwined with these arrangements. I need to discuss this with your father."

The following morning, Ahsan was summoned to his father's office, a practical space that reflected the nature of their family's business. The room was filled with maps, documents, and the occasional hint of industrial activity, with a large metal desk in the centre. As Ahsan entered, he saw his father seated behind the desk, the office's no-nonsense atmosphere mirroring Faraz Khan's pragmatic approach to both business and life.

"Ahsan," his father began, his voice firm but calm, "your mother has informed me about your feelings for Varda. This matter is not just about personal preferences; it affects family traditions and our relationship with Fazil Hussain's family. You must understand the gravity of this situation."

Ahsan nodded, his heart heavy. "I understand, Baba. I didn't want to cause any trouble, but I needed to be honest about my feelings."

His father leaned back in his chair; his expression thoughtful. "Tradition is important, but so is your happiness. I will confer with your brothers, and we will think as to how we can address this without causing unnecessary conflict."

Ahsan felt a mix of relief and apprehension. His father's willingness to discuss the matter was a small comfort, but the road ahead remained uncertain. As he left the office, he knew that the path to resolving this conflict would be fraught with challenges, but he was grateful that his family was willing to consider his feelings.

As he walked through the bustling streets of Kushalgram, the festive preparations seemed to mock his inner turmoil. Ahsan felt a flicker of hope amidst the uncertainty, knowing that his family's approach would play a crucial role in determining his future. The contrast between the external celebration and his internal conflict weighed heavily on him, but he was ready to face whatever came next with the hope that a resolution could be found that would respect both his heart and his family's traditions.

Later that night, Faraz Khan and his elder sons were locked in deep discussion. The atmosphere in the office was tense, with voices rising and falling as they debated the sudden turn of events. The elder brothers were staunchly opposed to any relationship with the Hussain family, less because of the rivalry and more due to their belief that Faraz Khan had given Ahsan too much freedom. They argued that this leniency had led to the current predicament.

As the night wore on, the discussions became more intense. Faraz Khan, although firm in his belief that his son's happiness was paramount, found himself navigating a delicate balance between tradition and modernity. The next morning, a decision was reached.

Faraz Khan and his wife would visit Fazil Hussain's house under the pretext of inviting him to their daughter's wedding. This visit would serve as a litmus test for the possibility of reconciling the two families.

The journey to Fazil Hussain's house was laden with tension. As they arrived, the surprised gasps of the Hussain family were audible. The sight of Faraz Khan, an unexpected guest, took them aback. Invitations to events between the rival families were rare, making this visit an unusual occurrence.

"Faraz Khan, what an unexpected pleasure," Fazil Hussain greeted warmly, masking his surprise with a courteous smile.

"We have come to invite you and your family to our daughter's wedding," Faraz Khan said, his tone respectful yet firm. "We hope you will join us in our celebration."

Fazil Hussain's eyes widened slightly, but he quickly composed himself. "Of course, we will be honoured to attend," he replied, extending his hand in a gesture of camaraderie.

The Khan couple was ushered inside, where they were served tea, rich sweets, and various refreshments. The hospitality was genuine, yet there was an underlying current of curiosity and speculation among the

Hussain family members. Conversations flowed, touching on various topics, but always skirting around the underlying tension.

"We will not just attend," Fazil Hussain declared with a smile. "My family and I will participate in the wedding chores. It will be a pleasure to be involved in such a joyous occasion."

Faraz Khan and his wife exchanged relieved glances, feeling a sense of hope. The hospitality and warm reception suggested an openness they had not anticipated. After a couple of hours, and much persuasion, they were finally allowed to leave, laden with good wishes and promises of participation.

As they drove back home, Faraz Khan's thoughts drifted to the previous night's discussions. His sons had been adamant, but the warm reception from the Hussains hinted at a possibility of reconciliation. Faraz and his wife felt a cautious optimism. They had planned that if Fazil Hussain agreed to attend the wedding festivities, they would propose the marriage of Ahsan and Varda during one of the pre-wedding events.

Back at home, the atmosphere was lighter. Both Faraz and his wife felt a sense of relief. The prospect of proposing the union during the wedding festivities seemed less daunting now. They knew the reaction of Fazil Hussain could go either way, but they were prepared to face it. For them, the happiness of their son was paramount, and they were determined to make the effort.

The Mehndi ceremony was held in the grand courtyard of the Khan residence, which had been transformed into a dazzling array of colours. Strings of marigold flowers draped from every conceivable surface, and fairy lights twinkled overhead, casting a warm, inviting glow. The scent of henna mingled with the aroma of delicious food, creating a festive atmosphere that was both vibrant and intoxicating. Women in traditional attire gathered around the bride, their laughter and song filling the air as intricate mehndi designs were applied.

The arrival of Fazil Hussain's family sent a ripple of surprise through the crowd. When they walked in, the chatter momentarily halted, and all eyes turned toward them. The sight of the rival family at such a joyful event was unexpected and piqued the curiosity of everyone present.

Varda, in particular, stood out amidst the celebrations. She wore a stunning dress with elaborate embroidery, her long hair cascading in soft waves. Her presence was captivating; her eyes sparkled with warmth and intelligence, and her smile was both shy and enchanting. The beauty she exuded drew admiration from everyone, and her grace was noted by all.

Ahsan, standing with his sisters and sister-in-law, couldn't take his eyes off her. His heart raced with a mix of excitement and nervousness. The teasing from his family began almost immediately.

"Look at him," his eldest sister said, her voice teasing. "He's so distracted by Varda, he might as well have a sign saying 'I'm in love'."

His younger sister joined in, "I think we should start taking bets on how long it will take him to actually speak to her. I'm guessing he'll turn into a statue before that happens."

Ahsan, feeling the heat of their scrutiny, tried to laugh it off. "Very funny. I'm just... admiring the atmosphere."

His sister-in-law added with a smirk, "Admiring the atmosphere, or admiring Varda? I think we know the answer!"

Their laughter and light-hearted teasing made Ahsan's face flush. Despite his embarrassment, he couldn't help but feel a surge of happiness. His family's support, though mischievous, was comforting.

Amidst the laughter, Ahsan's mother seized the moment to engage Varda in conversation. She approached Varda with a warm smile. "So, your name means 'Rose' in Arabic," she said, her tone gentle and inviting.

Varda nodded, her cheeks flushing slightly. "Yes, Auntie. It's an old family name."

Ahsan's mother smiled, genuinely impressed. "You are as beautiful and graceful as a rose, my dear. It's a pleasure to finally meet you. I've heard so much about you."

Varda's eyes widened in surprise, but she quickly recovered, offering a shy smile. "Thank you, Auntie. It's an honour to be here."

Meanwhile, the playful teasing from Ahsan's siblings continued unabated. His eldest sister leaned closer to him, whispering, "If you don't make a move soon, I think Varda might start thinking you're a statue."

His younger sister chimed in, "Or maybe she'll start thinking you're a permanent fixture of the decor."

Ahsan's sister-in-law added with a wink, "Come on, Ahsan, give us something to work with. You can't just stand here like a deer in headlights."

Despite their good-natured teasing, Ahsan felt a mixture of relief and amusement. His mother's intervention and the light-hearted banter from his siblings made him feel a bit more at ease. Though he remained frozen in place, his family's support and humour provided a comforting backdrop to his nervousness.

After dinner, Faraz Khan and his wife took Fazil Hussain and his wife aside, their expressions a blend of seriousness and nervous anticipation. Faraz Khan spoke carefully, "We have something to discuss. We know this may come as a surprise, but we would like to propose a marriage between Ahsan and Varda. There's no rush for the wedding; we'd be content with an engagement for now. We want you to know that whatever your decision, it won't affect our newfound friendship."

Fazil Hussain was momentarily stunned. He took a moment to collect his thoughts before responding. "This is unexpected, but we'll need some time to consider it."

Despite the initial shock, Fazil Hussain and his family left in good spirits, promising to be part of the next day's festivities. Faraz Khan and his wife felt a wave of relief at the positive reception. They knew that the proposal's outcome was uncertain, but they were satisfied that they had done their best for their son's happiness.

Chapter 2

The night following the Mehndi ceremony was a restless one for Fazil Hussain and his wife. They sat together in their modestly decorated living room, their faces etched with concern and contemplation. The proposal for their daughter Varda's marriage to Ahsan Faraz Khan had taken them by surprise, despite the underlying tensions between the families.

Fazil Hussain stared at the ceiling, his mind racing. He knew that Ahsan was a commendable match—his family was well-respected, and he had a solid reputation. Despite the ongoing rivalry between their families, the prospect of such a match was enticing. However, the unexpected nature of the proposal left him and his wife in a state of mental turmoil. They both understood the significance of this opportunity and the challenges it presented.

Fazil Hussain's wife, her brow furrowed with worry, broke the silence. "Fazil, this is a difficult situation. I know Ahsan is a good match, but what if Varda doesn't agree?"

"I understand," Fazil replied, his voice tinged with frustration. "But we need to consider Varda's feelings as well. She deserves to have a say in this decision."

The following morning, Varda was called into a private conversation with her parents. She walked into the room with a mixture of curiosity and apprehension, her expression calm but guarded. Her mother and father exchanged a glance before speaking.

"Varda," her mother began gently, "we need to discuss something important. Your father and I have received a proposal for your marriage to Ahsan Faraz Khan."

Varda's heart skipped a beat. She had heard of Ahsan, and she knew of the families' rivalry, but the proposal was unexpected. Her initial reaction was one of surprise and confusion.

"Do you know who Ahsan is?" her father asked, his tone firm but kind.

"Yes, Father," Varda replied, her voice barely above a whisper. "I've heard about him."

Her parents exchanged another look before her mother continued, "We believe that Ahsan is a good match for you. His family is highly respected, and despite the rivalry, we think this is a rare opportunity."

Varda struggled to find the right words. She wanted to voice her feelings, but she was conflicted. "I... I don't know, Mama. I appreciate the match, but... I can't give you a clear reason. I just feel unsure."

Her mother nodded, understanding the gravity of the situation. "We will respect your feelings, Varda. We'll give you some time to think about it. Your opinion matters to us."

After their discussion, Varda's parents were left in a state of contemplation. They decided that the best course of action was to formally accept the proposal, despite Varda's initial reluctance. They felt that the proposal was too significant to let slip away, and the potential benefits for their daughter's future were considerable.

That evening, the pre-wedding celebration dinner was held at Faraz Khan's residence. The atmosphere was filled with joyous anticipation as guests gathered to celebrate the upcoming marriage of Ahsan's elder sister. The tables were adorned with sumptuous dishes, and the air was alive with laughter and music.

As the guests mingled and enjoyed the festivities, Faraz Khan and his wife approached Fazil Hussain and his wife. The air was charged with excitement and a sense of formality.

Fazil Hussain greeted them with a warm but slightly reserved smile. "Faraz, it's good to see you again. The wedding is looking wonderful."

Faraz Khan smiled back, his eyes reflecting the warmth of their conversation. "Thank you, Fazil. We're delighted that you could join us tonight."

Taking a deep breath, Faraz Khan's wife spoke up, "Fazil Bhai, we wanted to let you know that we've been thinking about the proposal we discussed yesterday. We understand the complexity of the situation, but we truly believe that Ahsan and Varda would make a wonderful match. We hope that you and your family will consider this favourably."

Fazil Hussain looked at his wife, who gave a slight nod of encouragement. After a moment's hesitation, he spoke, "Faraz, after considering everything, we've decided to accept the proposal. We believe that despite our differences, this union has the potential to bring positive change."

A wave of relief washed over Faraz Khan and his wife. They extended their heartfelt thanks and promised that the formal engagement would be announced soon. The atmosphere of the dinner transformed into one of celebration as the news of the accepted proposal spread. Guests gathered around, offering their congratulations and sharing in the joyous occasion.

As the evening progressed, Varda joined the celebration. Despite her earlier reservations, she couldn't help but be moved by the warmth and acceptance she received from Ahsan's family. The sight of Ahsan, glowing with happiness, made her feel a mixture of emotions.

Ahsan's sisters and sister-in-law, having been in on the secret, playfully teased him throughout the evening. "Look at you, Ahsan," his younger sister said, "you're practically glowing. You're going to have to get used to this new normal!"

His sister-in-law added with a grin, "Now that the engagement is set, you'll have to stop acting like a lovesick puppy. It's time to step up!"

As the night drew to a close, the Faraz and Hussain families celebrated their new bond with heartfelt toasts and joyous laughter. The decision to announce the engagement and proceed with the formal ceremony was met with a collective sense of satisfaction and anticipation. Despite the hurdles that lay ahead, the families were united in their hope for a bright and harmonious future for Ahsan and Varda.

Chapter 3

As the sun began to set on the evening of the wedding, the atmosphere was electric with anticipation. Guests arrived at the beautifully decorated venue, which was adorned with intricate floral arrangements and twinkling fairy lights. The entire space had been transformed into a breathtaking setting for both the wedding and the engagement ceremony.

The wedding festivities were in full swing, with the vibrant colours of traditional attire blending harmoniously with the elegant decor. The aroma of delicious dishes wafted through the air, adding to the celebratory mood. Guests chatted animatedly, their faces lit with joy and excitement.

Amidst the preparations, the families were buzzing with activity. Varda, in her stunning bridal outfit, looked every bit the radiant bride. Her outfit was adorned with intricate embroidery and sparkling jewels, accentuating her graceful presence. Ahsan, dressed in a traditional sherwani, could hardly contain his happiness as he prepared for the dual ceremonies.

At Fazil Hussain's house, preparations for the announcement of the engagement were underway. Varda's family had been caught off guard by the proposal, and they had spent the morning deliberating over the unexpected turn of events. Varda's reluctance had added to their uncertainty, but after much consideration, they decided to proceed with the engagement. The decision was made, and they agreed to make the announcement alongside the wedding festivities.

As the evening progressed, the Nikah ceremony began. The solemn and beautiful ceremony was conducted with grace. The air was filled with a sense of reverence and joy as the couple exchanged vows, committing to their new life together.

After the Nikah, Faraz Khan and Fazil Hussain took the stage to address the guests. The crowd fell silent as Faraz Khan began to speak, his voice resonating with both pride and sincerity. He spoke of the joy and honour of having Fazil Hussain's family as part of the celebrations and revealed the surprise engagement of Ahsan and Varda. The announcement was met with a collective gasp of astonishment followed by a chorus of cheers and applause.

The guests were pleasantly surprised by the double celebration, and the mood shifted from initial shock to overwhelming delight. The engagement was seen as a significant step towards mending the rift between the two families, and it was clear that the tensions of the past were being set aside in favour of new beginnings.

The engagement ceremony was conducted with great pomp. Varda and Ahsan exchanged rings amidst a flurry of congratulations and good wishes from their families and friends. Despite Varda's initial reluctance, her smile, though shy, spoke volumes of her acceptance of the situation. She had agreed to the engagement, but there was a subtle hesitance in her manner, reflecting the complexity of her feelings.

As the event continued, Arun Kumar Singh, a distinguished officer from the Bureau of Cross-Border Trade Compliance and Integrity, made his way to the stage. Faraz Khan introduced him as a valued friend and a key figure in their professional world.

"Ahsan, Varda, I'd like you to meet Arun Kumar Singh ji, a distinguished officer from the Bureau of Cross-Border Trade Compliance and Integrity," Faraz Khan said.

Arun Kumar Singh addressed Faraz and Fazil with a warm "Faraz Bhai" and "Fazil Bhai," acknowledging their long-standing relationship. He then turned to Ahsan and Varda.

"Ahsan, Varda, I extend my heartfelt congratulations to you both," he said with a smile. "It's wonderful to see such a joyous union and the beginning of a new chapter."

Ahsan, beaming with pride, responded, "Thank you, Arun Uncle. It's great to have you here today."

Arun Kumar Singh's words and presence added a sense of formality and recognition to the celebrations, and his support further signified the positive turn in the relationship between the two families.

The night ended on a high note, with both families and guests celebrating the new alliances with dancing, music, and laughter. The engagement and wedding festivities symbolized a hopeful new beginning, bringing joy to all and paving the way for a harmonious future.

The next couple of days were very hectic for the family, filled with functions, lunches, and dinners to be attended at the in-laws of Ahsan's sister, Faraz's house, and Fazil's house. Amidst the hustle and bustle, Ahsan managed to corner his eldest sister and sisters-in-law, seeking their support to set up a private meeting with Varda and to seek permission from his mother and Varda's mother to connect with Varda on the phone.

His sister, and sisters-in-law couldn't help but tease him. "So our little Ahsan is finally growing up," his sister said, ruffling his hair.

"Ah, the young Romeo needs help to woo his Juliet," added his eldest sister in law with a chuckle.

The younger sister in law also joined in, "Don't worry, Ahsan. We'll make sure you don't mess it up... too much."

Blushing, Ahsan tried to defend himself, "I just want to talk to her, that's all."

They exchanged knowing glances and laughed. "Alright, alright," His sister said. "We'll help you. But you owe us, big time."

Ahsan's mother chimed in with a chuckle, "Leave the poor boy alone. He's head over heels in love. Let him have his moment."

Ahsan, desperate for some support, complained, "They're all harassing me, Ammi. Please, make them stop."

Chapter 4

After much playful banter and a bit of persuasion, they agreed to speak to their mother and Varda's mother. The mothers, amused by the situation, gave their consent, allowing Ahsan to connect with Varda on the phone.

When Ahsan finally called Varda, she was a bit aloof in her responses. He thought she was shy. "Hello, Varda. It's Ahsan," he began nervously.

"Hi, Ahsan," Varda replied softly.

"How are you?" Ahsan asked, trying to keep the conversation going.

"I'm fine. How are you?" she responded politely.

"I'm good, just busy with all the functions," Ahsan said, hoping to get more than one-word answers.

"Yes, it's been busy," Varda agreed.

Ahsan's sister, listening in on the conversation, couldn't resist making faces and whispering comments. "Ask her what her favourite colour is!".

"Tell her she has a nice voice," added her younger sister in law, pretending to swoon.

Trying to ignore his sisters' antics, Ahsan continued, "So, I was thinking... maybe we could talk more often?"

Varda hesitated. "Sure, that would be nice."

Ahsan's sister and sister in laws burst into silent laughter, their shoulders shaking with mirth. Finally, the call ended, and Ahsan felt a mixture of relief and confusion.

"She's just shy," his sister said, patting his back.

"Or maybe you're boring her to death," the elder sister in law teased.

The next day, before Ahsan was to travel to Kolkata and then further to Mumbai to undertake the formality of his Masters, he was allowed a meeting with Varda. He was to pick her up from her home, and they were allowed to have dinner together.

As Ahsan prepared for the date, his sisters and mother continued their playful teasing. "Make sure you don't wear that horrible cologne," his sister advised.

"Remember to compliment her dress," the elder sister in law added.

"And don't talk too much about yourself," the younger sister in law chimed in.

His mother, adding her bit, said humorously, "And remove that goofy smile from your face, Ahsan. You'll scare her away."

Ahsan, blushing furiously, scouted for the perfect gift. He finally settled on a beautiful necklace and a brand new cell phone, hoping they would impress Varda. He also decided to take her to a dress shop to buy her dresses of her choice.

When he arrived at Varda's house, his heart pounded with excitement. Varda, looking elegant and reserved, came out to meet him. As she sat on his bike, a wave of romanticism washed over him. The warmth of her presence and the delicate scent of her perfume filled the air.

They arrived at the dress shop, where Ahsan encouraged her to choose whatever she liked. Varda, still aloof, selected a few dresses with minimal conversation. He could sense her reluctance but attributed it to shyness.

For dinner, they went to a cozy restaurant. Ahsan presented her with the necklace and the cell phone, hoping to see a spark of excitement in her eyes. Varda smiled politely, accepting the gifts with a quiet "Thank you."

As they dined, Ahsan tried to engage her in light conversation, but Varda's responses remained brief. He kept telling himself she just needed time to open up.

After dinner, he dropped her back home. Varda hurried inside without saying goodnight, leaving Ahsan puzzled. "She's still shy," he thought, trying to reassure himself.

When he returned home, his sisters in law, sister and mother were waiting. "How did it go?" his sister asked eagerly.

"Did you scare her away with your goofy smile?" his mother added humorously.

Ahsan, feeling both amused and exasperated, recounted the evening. His sisters in law, his sister and mother couldn't stop laughing at his interpretations and reactions, making jokes and poking fun at every opportunity.

Early the next morning, Ahsan left for Kolkata, his heart a mix of hope and uncertainty about his future with Varda.

Chapter 5

Ahsan couldn't sleep the night before due to the excitement, so as soon as he boarded the train, he dozed off. The rhythmic clatter of the train wheels was usually soothing, but this time it couldn't keep his mind at ease for long. At around 11 a.m., his phone rang, waking him from a fitful sleep. Smiling, he took out his phone, thinking it was a call from Varda. His heart skipped a beat, only for his hopes to crash when he saw his eldest brother's name on the screen.

"Hello, Bhai!" he greeted cheerfully, but his brother's response was a barrage of expletives.

"You idiot, you perv, bastard! You couldn't control yourself? It was you who created this pretence of getting married late. We were ready to get you married, and you did this? Are you out of your freaking mind?" his brother yelled, his voice filled with anger and disgust.

Ahsan was taken aback, unable to understand what he had done. All he could muster was, "Bhai, what? Bhai, I don't understand."

"Stop being so naive!" his brother snapped. "The cheap antics you tried with Varda have got us all in grievous trouble. You tried to get physical with her, and when she resisted, you verbally abused her and her family and threatened to break off the engagement."

Ahsan was in shock, struggling to comprehend what his brother was saying. "I never did anything like that!" he protested, his voice shaking with desperation.

But his brother continued, "Fazil Hussain has broken off the engagement and has threatened to file a police case as well. The wedge that was supposed to be filled has become deeper, thanks to you. Our family is in turmoil because of your actions. Baba is very angry and won't even speak with you."

Ahsan felt a sinking feeling in his stomach. He tried to explain his side, but his brother wouldn't listen. "You need to stay put in Kolkata, get a new phone, and wait for further instructions," his brother ordered.

Ahsan suggested coming back to Kushalgram to sort things out, but his brother stopped him. "Police action is something we can manage, but knowing Fazil Hussain, he would take matters into his own hands and get justice for his daughter by bypassing the law. It's safer for you to stay away."

Ahsan felt tears prickling at the corners of his eyes. "Bhai, please, you have to believe me. I didn't do anything wrong. I love Varda," he pleaded, but his brother's voice remained cold and distant.

"Just do as you're told, Ahsan," his brother said before abruptly hanging up the phone.

Feeling isolated and helpless, Ahsan tried calling his mother, Baba, and sisters, but no one picked up his calls. Each unanswered ring felt like a punch to his gut. The rest of his journey to Kolkata was one of the most stressful experiences of his life. He stared out of the train window, the passing landscapes a blur as his mind raced with thoughts of what could have possibly gone wrong.

Once he reached Kolkata, he removed his SIM card, bought a new one, and called his brother to inform him. His brother curtly acknowledged the information and disconnected the call without any further talk, leaving Ahsan in a state of emotional limbo.

Wandering the bustling streets of Kolkata, Ahsan felt a profound sense of loneliness. The city was vibrant and alive, but he felt detached from it all, burdened by the accusations and the broken trust of his family. He found a small, nondescript hotel to stay in and checked into a room, collapsing onto the bed with a heavy heart.

As he lay there, Ahsan replayed the events of the past few days in his mind. The joyful wedding, the surprise engagement, the fleeting moments of happiness with Varda—everything seemed like a distant dream now turned into a nightmare. He couldn't fathom how things had spiralled out of control so quickly.

"Why would Varda make such an allegation?" he pondered. The confusion gnawed at him. He had been nothing but respectful during their brief interactions. The night of their first date replayed in his mind over and over. They had gone to dinner, he had given her a beautiful necklace and a brand-new cell phone, and though she seemed a bit aloof, he chalked it up to shyness. He hadn't even touched her, let alone behaved inappropriately. Ahsan couldn't comprehend why she would accuse him of something so heinous.

In the silence of his room, Ahsan made a vow to clear his name and mend the rift between the families. He needed to understand why Varda would lie about him. Could there be another motive? Was someone else influencing her? His mind spun with questions, but for now, he had to wait, uncertain of what the future held and how he would navigate the turbulent waters that lay ahead.

Chapter 6

After returning from the dinner with Ahsan, Varda went straight to her room. She looked tired, so her mother didn't probe her further about the dinner, thinking she would take all the details the next day.

The next morning, Varda's mother was busy in the kitchen, preparing breakfast. She called out to Varda, her voice laced with a hint of frustration. "Varda, wake up! You need to get your schedule right now that you're going to get married!"

When Varda didn't come down after some time, her mother, grumbling under her breath about Varda's lack of punctuality, decided to go upstairs to her room. She called out from outside the door but received no response. Growing worried, she opened the door and was met with a horrifying sight.

Varda was semi-conscious, lying in a pool of her own blood, a blade lying next to her. Panic surged through her mother as she rushed to Varda's side, her mind racing to comprehend what had happened. The once bustling morning had turned into a scene of chaos and dread.

Varda was rushed to the hospital. After a thorough examination, the doctors felt a sense of relief. It was out of sheer luck that her artery was intact; only the upper part of her skin was damaged. Due to the loss of blood, she was unconscious. Fazil Hussain and his family were deeply worried, unable to understand why their beloved daughter would take such a step. They decided to keep the incident under wraps, fearing the social stigma it might bring.

After some time, Varda regained consciousness. Her mother was sitting by her side, her face a mixture of relief and concern. She gently asked everyone else to leave the room so she could speak freely with her daughter.

Varda's mother leaned in close, her voice soft and tender. "My dear Varda, you scared us all so much. What happened? Why would you do this to yourself?" She stroked Varda's hair gently, her eyes filled with tears. "You can tell me anything, my love. I'm here for you, always."

Varda's eyes filled with tears as she looked at her mother. The emotional burden she had been carrying for so long was finally too heavy to bear. "Ammi, it was Ahsan," she began, her voice trembling. "He tried to get physical with me. When I refused, he abused me and our family. He threatened to break off the engagement and malign us. I was so scared and didn't know what else to do. I thought if I... if I ended my life, it would save our family's honour."

Her mother's heart broke at hearing these words. She embraced Varda, holding her close. "Oh, my sweet child. You should have told us. We would have protected you. No one should ever make you feel this way."

When Fazil Hussain learned about the revelation, a storm of fury overtook him. He was a man known for his composure, but this was too much to bear. He immediately called Faraz Khan to the hospital, his voice barely restrained. "Faraz, you need to come to the hospital now. We have a serious matter to discuss regarding your son."

Faraz Khan arrived quickly, his face etched with concern. Fazil Hussain wasted no time, recounting the entire episode in detail. Shock and disbelief spread across Faraz's face as he listened. "Ahsan is on a train to Kolkata," he muttered.

Fazil's anger only grew. "Your son has dishonoured my daughter and threatened my family. I am publicly breaking off this engagement. If you do not take immediate action, I will pursue legal recourse against Ahsan and your entire family."

The public announcement of the broken engagement reverberated through the community. Fazil Hussain's voice was filled with authority and indignation as he made the declaration, ensuring everyone knew the reasons behind it. His resolve to protect his daughter's honour and seek justice was clear. The threat of legal action underscored the gravity of the situation, sending a powerful message that such behaviour would not be tolerated.

Faraz Khan and his family were distraught. They had always believed in Ahsan's character, but he had been away from home for the last five to six years. Who knew what lay behind that seemingly innocent exterior? Regardless, he was their son, and in the eyes of the community, he was guilty unless proven otherwise. With the threat of legal consequences hanging over them, they had to act swiftly.

Firstly, they needed to ensure Ahsan stayed away from Kushalgram. With Fazil Hussain's connections, it was only a matter of time before he tracked Ahsan through his cell phone and possibly hired someone to physically harm him. Faraz Khan was acutely aware of the lengths Fazil might go to in order to protect his family's honour.

Faraz gathered his family in the living room, his face grim. "We need to make sure Ahsan stays hidden. Fazil will stop at nothing to find him, and I can't risk that. Our first priority is his safety."

He turned to his eldest son, his expression hardening. "Call Ahsan. Tell him to hide, to go somewhere no one can find him. Make it clear that I am not interested in speaking with him now or in the future."

His eldest son hesitated, the weight of the situation pressing down on him. "But Baba, where should he go? How will he manage?"

Faraz's voice was stern and unwavering. "That is for him to figure out. He has put us all in danger, and now he must face the consequences of his actions. Tell him to use cash, avoid using his phone, and stay off the grid. He cannot afford to be found."

With a heavy heart, his eldest son dialled Ahsan's number.

As his eldest son ended the call, the gravity of the situation settled over the family. Faraz Khan's heart ached with a mixture of anger and sorrow. He had to protect his family, even if it meant pushing his son away. The threat of Fazil's wrath and the potential legal consequences loomed large, and their only option was to ensure Ahsan stayed hidden and out of reach.

Varda's Story

Varda returned home from the dinner with Ahsan, her mind buzzing with conflicting emotions. Ahsan was kind, respectful, and came from a family that held a significant position in Kushalgram. But her heart had long belonged to Ifzal, her sister-in-law's brother. For three years, she and Ifzal had kept their relationship a secret, waiting for him to finish his education, get settled professionally, before making their intentions known to their families.

The sudden proposal from Ahsan's family had thrown everything into disarray. Her parents had accepted it without hesitation, and the engagement was already in motion. The shock of the situation left both Varda and Ifzal reeling. They had dreamed of a future together, and now that future seemed to be slipping away.

One evening, Ifzal, determined not to lose Varda, suggested an idea that initially left her stunned. It was bold, risky, and could potentially hurt many people, including Ahsan. But as days passed, Varda began to see the logic behind Ifzal's suggestion. Her love for him was strong, and the thought of losing him pushed her to consider the plan more seriously.

The dinner date with Ahsan provided the perfect opportunity for Varda to set Ifzal's plan in motion. She felt a pang of guilt for Ahsan, who was an innocent party in this intricate web of emotions. Yet, her love for Ifzal overshadowed her hesitation. She knew that to be with the one she truly loved, she had to take a leap of faith.

During the dinner, as Ahsan spoke about their potential future together, Varda's mind was elsewhere, calculating the steps she needed to take. She played along, giving him the responses he wanted to hear, while internally preparing for the drastic measures that awaited.

Varda feigned tiredness and went to her room early that evening. Restlessness consumed her throughout the night as she wrestled with the gravity of what she was about to do. In the early hours of the morning, she lay awake, waiting for her mother to call her for breakfast.

As expected, her mother called out to her. Varda remained silent, listening intently. Her mother called again, but still, Varda didn't answer. The execution of her plan required her mother to come to her room. She knew her mother's concern would drive her upstairs after receiving no response.

When she felt the time was right, Varda took a deep breath and picked up the blade she had hidden under her pillow. With deft accuracy, she made precise cuts to her wrist, ensuring they were deep enough to bleed profusely but not fatal. She made sure the bedsheet was stained with blood, creating a dramatic scene. Her heart raced as she lay down, waiting for her mother to enter.

Moments later, Varda's mother, growing increasingly worried, climbed the stairs and called out once more. Still, there was no answer. Fear gripped her as she opened the door and rushed into the room. The sight before her was horrifying; Varda lay semi-conscious in a pool of her own blood, the blade lying next to her.

Chapter 7

The next few days were the toughest for Faraz Khan and his family. The household was engulfed in a cloud of stress and anxiety, grappling with the stigma of their son's alleged act and the fallout that came with it. The tension was palpable, and the atmosphere within the house was heavy with unspoken fears and worries.

Faraz Khan's usually bustling home had become eerily quiet. His wife was often found weeping silently in a corner, struggling to understand how their son could have caused such turmoil. His elder sons, who usually managed the family business with confidence and ease, were now preoccupied and tense, their conversations hushed and filled with concern. The sisters were equally affected, torn between their love for their brother and the shame that now seemed to envelop the family.

Friends and acquaintances began to keep their distance, whispers of the incident spreading like wildfire through Kushalgram. The family felt the sting of social stigma, their once respected name now under a shadow. Faraz Khan himself was a man torn apart, struggling to maintain his composure. His anger towards Ahsan was mixed with a profound sense of betrayal and sorrow. He had always taken pride in his children, and this situation had shattered that pride into pieces.

Meanwhile, Ahsan was experiencing a different kind of torment. Isolated and alone, he moved from one anonymous place to another, trying to stay hidden. The loneliness was suffocating, and the silence of his family was even more painful than the physical isolation. He tried calling his family members repeatedly, desperate to explain his side, to hear a familiar voice, but no one answered. Each unanswered call deepened his despair and sense of abandonment.

His mind was a whirlpool of fear and confusion. Ahsan replayed the events in his head over and over, trying to understand where things had gone wrong. The accusations felt surreal, like a nightmare he couldn't wake up from. He missed the warmth of his home, the laughter of his siblings, and the comfort of his mother's presence. Now, all he had was the cold reality of his situation and the haunting uncertainty of what lay ahead.

On the fifth day, Ahsan's phone rang. His heart raced as he saw it was his elder brother calling. Hope surged within him as he answered the call. "Bhai, please listen to me, I didn't do anything wrong. You have to believe me!"

His brother's voice was curt and emotionless. "Ahsan, there's no time for explanations. You need money for your daily expenses. Go to the address I'm sending you now. There will be an envelope with cash. Take it and stay hidden. Do not contact us; we will contact you as and when required."

"But Bhai, please! I need to talk to someone; I need to explain—"

The line went dead. Ahsan stared at his phone. The brief conversation had only added to his anguish. The coldness in his brother's voice, the lack of any warmth or reassurance, cut him deeply. He felt abandoned, cast out by his own family, left to fend for himself in a world that now seemed overwhelmingly hostile.

With no other choice, Ahsan followed his brother's instructions and made his way to the small, nondescript jewellery store. The shop was an old, unremarkable building nestled among more prominent businesses, its faded sign barely noticeable. Inside, the store was dimly lit, showcasing various pieces of jewellery behind glass counters. The shopkeeper, a middle-aged man with a stern expression, looked up as Ahsan entered.

Ahsan approached the counter and introduced himself quietly. The shopkeeper nodded briefly, his eyes assessing Ahsan with a professional detachment. Without a word, the shopkeeper reached under the counter and pulled out a plain envelope. He handed it to Ahsan with a simple, almost mechanical gesture.

Ahsan took the envelope, feeling the weight of its contents, and tucked it into his pocket. The shopkeeper's silence spoke volumes, reflecting the gravity of the situation and the unspoken understanding between them. Ahsan left the store with the envelope in hand, each step echoing the heavy sense of isolation that now enveloped him.

The envelope contained enough cash to cover his immediate needs, but it did little to alleviate the crushing loneliness and despair that weighed on him. The isolation was a constant, gnawing presence, and the reality of his situation seemed to deepen with each passing day. Ahsan's routine became a monotonous cycle of hiding, moving from one anonymous place to another, always on the lookout for potential danger or recognition. He avoided public areas as much as possible, relying on cash transactions to maintain a low profile. Each night was a sleepless vigil, and each day brought a new wave of uncertainty and fear.

Back at home, Faraz Khan and his family were also grappling with the fallout. The stress of the situation had taken a severe toll on their emotional and physical well-being. The once vibrant home now felt like a shadow of its former self, with every corner echoing the silent strains of their collective anguish. The social stigma and the weight of their son's actions loomed over them, creating a chasm between the family members and leaving them to navigate a treacherous landscape of mistrust and sorrow.

After his brother's curt phone call, Ahsan ceased all attempts to contact his other family members, coming to terms with the fact that he was no longer desired by anyone in the family except for his mother. Despite the cold reception from his siblings and the distant nature of his father, he continued to reach out to her in a gesture of hope and connection.

Each day, Ahsan made it a point to call his mother three times—just a single ring each time. He would do this in the morning when he woke up, in the afternoon after lunch, and in the evening before going for dinner. These brief calls were his way of letting her know that he was still alive and managing, despite the harsh circumstances.

He didn't expect her to answer or engage in conversation; the rings were more of a symbolic gesture, a way to maintain a thread of communication, however tenuous. Each call was a small affirmation of his ongoing existence and a silent plea for her to understand the depth of his anguish. Even though these calls were often met with silence, they were his way of staying connected to the family he felt increasingly estranged from.

It was the 17th day since Ahsan had left Kushalgram. Though he had been living away from his family for over five years, this time felt different. He was feeling slightly under the weather that morning. After lunch, he visited a local chemist, picked up a tablet for fever, and returned to his modest hotel room, planning to lie down for a bit before making his usual call to his mother.

However, the fever and the emotional distress had taken a greater toll on him than he realized. Exhausted, he slipped into a fitful and dreamless sleep. The room was silent and dark when he woke up, drenched in sweat and overwhelmed by an intense thirst. Disoriented, he struggled to understand where he was and what time it was.

After a few disoriented minutes, he managed to gather his senses. Outside, the darkness was deep and unyielding. He checked his mobile and was astonished to see that it was 4 a.m. He had slept for over 12 hours. To his surprise, there were 10 missed calls from his mother. The joy he felt was overwhelming, his emotions surging through him as he cried out in relief.

He wanted to call her immediately, but he realized it was still too early. He decided to wait for a few more hours before returning her call. The anticipation of speaking with her, hearing her voice after so many days of silence, filled him with a bittersweet hope. As he lay back down, he allowed himself a brief moment of comfort, holding onto the warmth of the connection that those missed calls represented.

Ahsan didn't have to wait long. At around 6:30 a.m., his phone rang once again. The number flashing on the screen brought a rare, hopeful smile to his face. The display indicated that Ammi was calling. He answered the call with a trembling hand, his heart pounding with anticipation.

As he heard his mother's voice on the other end, he could sense the emotions she was trying to contain. Her voice wavered slightly, as though she was making a conscious effort to hold back her tears. The sight of her name on the screen had already brought him immense comfort, but hearing her voice now was like a balm to his aching soul.

"Ahsan?" she said softly, her voice choked with emotion. "How are you? Are you alright?"

The question brought tears to Ahsan's eyes. He struggled to find his voice but was overcome by a wave of sobs. His response was a series of soft, broken sobs that conveyed the depth of his longing and the immense joy he felt at hearing her voice. Words were inadequate to express the complexity of his emotions, so he let his tears speak for him.

His mother, sensing his distress and the overwhelming emotion, tried to keep the conversation light and reassuring. "I've been so worried about you," she said gently. "Are you eating well? Are you taking care of yourself?"

Ahsan managed a few words between his sobs. "Yes, Ammi. I'm... managing. Just... a bit sick, but... I'm fine." The words came out haltingly, his voice cracking with the strain of trying to stay composed.

She continued, trying to maintain a semblance of normalcy, "I've been praying for you every day. I miss you so much. I hope you know that we're all thinking about you."

They spoke for about five minutes, skirting around the main issues and avoiding any direct mention of the troubling circumstances that had led to his current situation. Their conversation was a delicate dance of reassurances and unspoken fears. They both knew that discussing the full scope of his troubles was too dangerous and would risk drawing unwanted attention.

As the conversation drew to a close, his mother's voice grew more cautious. "I need to go now," she said, her voice strained with the effort of keeping her emotions in check. "I'll call you again soon, Insha Allah. Take care of yourself, my dear."

Ahsan's heart felt a pang of sadness as the call ended. He wanted to say more, to tell her everything, but the fear of being overheard made it impossible. He promised himself that he would cherish these moments of connection, however brief they were. As the call disconnected, he lay back down, the warmth of the conversation lingering with him, a small beacon of hope in the midst of his isolation.

Indeed, Ahsan's mother called him back, and this time the conversation was more composed, though the underlying sadness still lingered. The initial tearful exchange had given way to a more regular pattern of communication. They spoke two to three times a day, their conversations becoming a small lifeline for both.

It wasn't until the fifth day that Ahsan mustered the courage to discuss the incident that had led to his exile. He had been anxiously awaiting the right moment, but the weight of his uncertainty and the need for answers drove him to finally broach the topic. When he asked his mother about the events, she initially tried to deflect, her voice trembling as she attempted to avoid the painful subject.

However, Ahsan's insistence finally broke through his mother's resistance. With a heavy heart, she revealed the devastating news. Varda had attempted suicide, and had blamed Ahsan for everything. This revelation shook Ahsan to his core. The sense of guilt and helplessness he felt was overwhelming.

His mother continued, her voice breaking, "Varda did survive the attempt, though. She was discharged from the hospital the next day. But the damage was done, and the repercussions were severe."

The news that Varda had survived but still faced significant repercussions added another layer of anguish for Ahsan. The guilt over her suffering and the subsequent fallout was a burden he struggled to bear, further deepening his isolation and distress.

Ahsan's mother continued, her voice breaking, "It took a lot of persuasion from your father, the local community members, and even Arun Kumar Singh to convince Fazil Hussain not to file a police complaint against you. It was a terrible situation."

She explained that Fazil Hussain had imposed stern conditions. Chief among them was that Ahsan would never be allowed to return to Kushalgram. The attempt on Varda's life had severely damaged her reputation, making it nearly impossible to find another match for her.

In a surprising turn, Ifzal's family stepped forward, announcing that he was ready to marry Varda. This move was seen as a gesture of goodwill and an attempt to salvage Varda's reputation. However, Fazil Hussain had one more condition: Faraz Khan was to bear the expenses of Varda's and Ifzal's marriage and, in addition, pay another 25 lacs as financial compensation for the mental anguish caused by Ahsan's actions.

Faced with no other viable options and concerned for his son's well-being, Faraz Khan reluctantly agreed to the terms. The marriage was set to take place in four days.

Despite the resolution, whispered rumours about Varda and Ifzal's college romance persisted. These rumours suggested that Varda and Ifzal had a pre-existing relationship, which only added to the suspicion that Ahsan had been framed. Faraz Khan's family suspected this might be the case, but without concrete evidence, they were unable to refute the allegations directly.

The situation left Faraz Khan's family in a grim position, grappling with the fallout from the scandal while shouldering both emotional and financial burdens. The financial costs—covering Varda's and Ifzal's wedding expenses, along with the additional 25 lacs in compensation—were a heavy strain. The emotional stress had taken its toll on every member of the family, deepening their resentment and anger towards Ahsan.

Faraz Khan's sons, who had been opposed to Ahsan's bond with Varda from the very beginning, now harboured a permanent sense of bitterness and anger. The scandal and its consequences had only reinforced their negative feelings, creating a deep rift and ongoing tension between them and Ahsan. Their anger was not just at Ahsan but also at the entire situation, which they felt had been mishandled and had ultimately led to a series of damaging outcomes for the family.

Ahsan's mother tried to reassure him, her voice filled with maternal love and concern. "Don't worry," she said gently. "It will take time, but things will eventually turn back to normalcy." Despite her comforting words, Ahsan knew deep down that her assurances were more a reflection of her motherly affection and hope than any real certainty about the future.

They spoke for a little while longer, though Ahsan couldn't recall the specifics of their conversation—his mind was too clouded with a sense of despair and confusion. When the call ended, he was left alone with his thoughts, the weight of the situation pressing heavily upon him.

He stood up from his bed, walked to the window, and fiercely gripped the railing. The cool metal felt solid and unyielding in his hands, a stark contrast to the turmoil within him. With a muted scream, he let out his pent-up frustration and grief. His head hit the heavy window railing with a dull thud, the physical pain momentarily overshadowing the emotional agony. The act was a raw expression of his helplessness, a silent cry for relief from the crushing burden he carried.

After a while, Ahsan managed to collect himself. He stumbled to the bathroom, turned on the shower, and let the cold water cascade over him. The chilling splash of water was both jarring and invigorating, cutting through the haze of his emotions and the lingering sense of despair. He stood under the shower, letting the cold water wash away the remnants of his earlier breakdown.

Chapter 8

When he emerged from the bathroom, the person who stepped out was markedly different from the one who had entered. The earlier feelings of love, affection, and helplessness—emotions that had contributed to his current predicament—were replaced by a cold, unyielding fury. The water had cleansed him not just physically but emotionally, leaving behind a steely resolve.

Gone was the man who had been emotionally vulnerable and conflicted. In his place was a figure driven by a hardened sense of anger and resentment. His feelings toward Varda, his father, and to some extent his brothers had transformed into a simmering rage. He felt betrayed and wronged, and this new, fierce determination marked a significant shift in his outlook as he confronted the stark reality of his situation.

Ahsan sat at the edge of the bed, his mind a whirl of deep, logical thought. The wrongs done to him were clear, and the purpose of his anger was now unmistakable. Only the path to vengeance was shrouded in uncertainty, but this did not trouble him. He knew that his cold fury and rightly directed anger would illuminate the way. The longer it took to exact his revenge, the greater the satisfaction it would ultimately grant.

As he contemplated his course of action, a singular thought crystallized in his mind. He resolved, with a steely determination, that in the cold darkness of betrayal, revenge was the flame that would light his path—slow, fierce, and utterly consuming.

By late night, Ahsan's plan was etched clearly in his mind, the details meticulously mapped out. He set the execution date for the day before

Varda's marriage to Ifzal. The time for revenge was drawing near, and every step was carefully calculated.

As the first step in his plan, Ahsan decided to contact his brother. He sent a message rather than making a call, knowing that this method would create a record of his request. He wrote:

"Urgent: I need money urgently. My savings are depleted due to a medical emergency, and I am under significant debt. Please assist me as soon as possible."

The message was crafted to sound genuine and desperate, ensuring that his brother would take it seriously and respond promptly.

By the next morning, Ahsan received a call from his brother but chose not to answer. Instead, he sent a message, stating he was unable to speak and asked his brother to text him. His brother, concerned, inquired about the amount of money needed.

Ahsan replied with a carefully crafted story: "I've been hospitalized, and the bills from the hospital and medical store have come to Rs. 1.5 lacs. I would need at least 2.5 lacs to cover all expenses."

His brother, assessing the situation, asked if Ahsan would be able to collect the money. Ahsan confirmed that he could. His brother then instructed him to go to the same jeweller where he had collected money before and pick up 3 lacs this time.

Ahsan responded with a terse but affirmative, "Ok."

Ahsan's mother was clearly annoyed and hurt that he had concealed his hospitalization from her. Her voice was tinged with concern as she expressed her frustration.

"You should have told me you were in the hospital," she said. "I was worried sick."

Ahsan apologized sincerely, trying to calm her down. "I'm sorry, Ammi. I didn't want to add to your worries. I thought it would be better if you didn't know."

He reassured her, “Please don’t worry about me. I can take care of myself. I’m managing just fine.”

Despite his reassurances, his mother insisted on coming to Kolkata to be with him. But Ahsan declined her offer, emphasizing that he was capable of handling the situation on his own. “No, Ammi. Whatever happens, I’ll always look after myself. I need you to stay there and not get involved in this.”

As their conversation continued, Ahsan, feeling a twinge of curiosity and caution, asked, “Is anyone in the family aware of our conversations?”

His mother responded with a firm and reassuring negative. “No, no one knows I’m talking to you. I’ve kept this between us.”

Ahsan, though still feeling the weight of his situation, took some comfort in her answer. The conversation ended with a promise to keep in touch, but he remained focused on his plans, knowing that his path to revenge was drawing closer.

Chapter 9

The long-awaited day had arrived. Ahsan woke up early, feeling the weight of his plans pressing down on him. He took a shower, dressed carefully and left his hotel room.

Ahsan's next stop was the Vidyasagar Bridge, a place he had chosen for its strategic significance. He walked up and down the bridge several times, meticulously checking every corner and crevice. He needed to be certain that everything was in place and that the bridge would serve its purpose effectively. Once he was satisfied with his assessment, he decided to have lunch.

The bustling city around him contrasted sharply with the focus and intensity that Ahsan felt. As he ate, he reflected on the final stages of his plan, mentally preparing himself for the crucial tasks ahead.

After a late lunch, he headed to the restaurant counter and used the hotel's guest landline phone to make a crucial call.

With a mix of apprehension and resolve, Ahsan dialled his father's number. When his father, Faraz Khan, answered, Ahsan was struck by the distant tone in his voice. He greeted him formally, "Baba, Assalamoalaikum. Ahsan here."

The reaction was immediate and fierce. Faraz's voice, though calm, was seething with barely contained rage. "I think it was made very clear to you that you are no longer to keep in contact with us until instructed otherwise."

Ahsan attempted to explain and calm his father, but his efforts were in vain. Faraz's anger was palpable, and without giving Ahsan a chance to respond further, he abruptly disconnected the call. Ahsan was left with a sense of despair, the gravity of his father's reaction sinking in deeply.

Unperturbed and with a steely resolve, Ahsan dialled Varda's number next.

Although the atmosphere of the wedding was more about relief than joy—highlighting the fact that someone was ready to accept Varda as his bride rather than celebrating a new chapter in her life—Varda felt a deep sense of happiness within. She was finally going to be with Ifzal forever. The presence of Ahsan, who had once been an obstacle in their love story, was now a thing of the past. She had convinced herself that everything that happened to Ahsan and his family was a consequence of their own actions. They had interfered in her love story, and now they were paying the price.

In the midst of these thoughts, Varda's cell phone buzzed. It was the same phone Ahsan had gifted her—a keepsake she had chosen not to part with due to its expensive price tag. The number was unknown. Initially, she ignored the call, but the phone buzzed again. Irritated, she ignored it once more, but when it buzzed a third time, her patience wore thin. She answered the call, ready to give a scolding to whoever was bothering her with what she presumed to be a promotional call.

"Hello," she said irritably.

The voice on the other end was cold and steely, yet unmistakably familiar.

"I believe congratulations are in order, Varda," Ahsan said, his tone carrying a chilling edge. "History says that to achieve something monumental, sacrifices must be made. I feel honoured to have been the chosen one to be sacrificed for the culmination of your love story with Ifzal. Here's congratulations once again. May you live in interesting times." And the call was disconnected.

The words hit Varda like a cold gust of wind, and she was left grappling with a mixture of shock and unease. But she decided to keep mum, no sense getting her family members worried about this nuisance phone call.

Just half an hour before sunset, Ahsan arrived at Vidyasagar Bridge once again. The fading light of the day cast long shadows, adding an eerie atmosphere to the scene.

He took out his cell phone and began recording the video he had rehearsed for the past two days. With a calm and deliberate manner, he spoke into the camera, his words measured and his tone steady. The video was a crucial part of his plan, designed to communicate his message clearly and effectively.

As he spoke, the camera captured the bridge's iconic arches and the darkening sky, framing his words with a dramatic backdrop. Each sentence was carefully crafted to ensure that his message would be delivered exactly as intended, leaving no room for misinterpretation.

Satisfied with the video, Ahsan carefully inserted his original SIM card back into his phone. He switched it on and sent the video to his brothers, sisters, father, Fazil Hussain, Varda, and their family lawyer. Each recipient would receive the message he had meticulously prepared.

After sending the video, Ahsan transferred it to his new phone, which he had purchased just a day before. The new phone chimed as the video was received, and he checked it once more to ensure it had transferred correctly. Satisfied with the result, he took a deep breath.

With a final glance at his old phone, which had served him through many trials, and a pair of old shoes, he tossed both into the river. The items floated away, symbols of his past and the end of a chapter.

As night began to settle, the emergency police number rang. The operator on the other end of the line was greeted by a breathless, middle-aged man with an Anglo-Indian accent. The caller reported urgently that someone had just jumped off Vidyasagar Bridge. He explained that he had been jogging when he saw a young man climbing over the bridge's railing. Despite his efforts to intervene, the man had already jumped by the time he reached him.

The operator, trying to gather more information, asked for the caller's identity. The response came back as disjointed and incoherent, filled with gibberish, before the call abruptly disconnected.

Ahsan, who had made the call from a public phone booth, quickly removed the additional padding from his mouth, which he had used to alter his voice. He discarded it outside the booth and hailed a taxi. As the taxi sped away into the encroaching darkness, Ahsan disappeared into the night, his plan set into motion.

The video that Ahsan sent proved to be a bombshell. It was a video graphic suicide note in a sense. Shot near the railing of the bridge, he began by apologizing to his friends and family in general and his parents in particular.

"I am deeply sorry for what I am about to do," he started, his voice steady but filled with sorrow. "I apologize for committing this act. I apologize for falling in love with Varda. I apologize for unknowingly blemishing my family's reputation. But before I die, I need to come clean."

He clarified his stand: "I never tried to hurt Varda. I loved her deeply, and my intentions were always pure. The accusations against me are false. I was framed, and the truth was twisted beyond recognition. I did not try to get physical with Varda, nor did I threaten her or her family. The events of that evening have been grossly misrepresented."

Addressing Varda, his voice softened, "Varda, I loved you with all my heart. I respected you and never meant to cause you any harm. I can't understand why you would accuse me of such horrendous things.

Turning his attention to Fazil Hussain, he said, "Fazil Uncle, you should have at least heard my side of the story before going all out against my family. You should seek proof from Varda about my alleged misdeeds, I have the confidence that there will be none. The timeline of that evening, as per my recollection, has been twisted beyond belief.

I am deeply disappointed in you for putting forth so many conditions to not file a police complaint. My family fulfilled all your demands, yet you still sent three contract killers after me. How did you get my cell phone location despite no police complaint being filed? This clearly indicates the involvement of corrupt policemen who used state machinery against me."

Lastly, he expressed his love for his parents, his voice breaking, "Ammi, Baba, I love you both more than anything in this world. I am sorry for the pain and disgrace my actions have caused you. I wish I could have cleared my name and spared you this suffering. But I can't go on like this.

Varda, Fazil Hussain, the corrupt policemen, and the three contract killers are the one's responsible for my suicide.

His final words were a poignant mixture of love and despair, "I hope my death will bring some peace to all those who have wronged me. Maybe in the end, justice will be served. Farewell."

With that, Ahsan ended the recording.

Chapter 10

Varda stared at the screen, watching the video Ahsan had sent her just before his death. As his final, desperate words echoed in the room, she felt nothing but irritation. How dare he try to make his death her burden? How dare he disrupt her life with his weak, pathetic display? In her mind, Ahsan's suicide was nothing more than an act of cowardice, and she resented him for it. She had no time for remorse, no space for sorrow. All she saw was someone who couldn't handle the reality of the world—a world where only the strong and self-assured like her could thrive. To Varda, Ahsan's death was his own fault, and she felt no guilt, only contempt for his weakness.

The entire town and the government machinery were in disarray. Suddenly, Ahsan had become the victim, and everyone felt sorry that they were taken for a ride by the wrongful behaviour of Varda and her father. Whispers and murmurs of regret filled the streets of Kushalgram. Those who once shunned Ahsan's family now looked at them with a mix of sympathy and shame.

The shocking revelations in Ahsan's video sparked widespread outrage. People began questioning the integrity of those they once respected. The town's perception of Varda and her father, Fazil Hussain, shifted dramatically. Once seen as upright members of society, they were now the focal point of public scorn. Parents forbade their children from associating with Varda's family, and local businesses severed ties with Fazil Hussain, fearing the backlash of being connected to such deceit.

In response to the uproar, a high-level inquiry was ordered to investigate whether government machinery was indeed misused to pinpoint Ahsan's phone location. The investigation moved swiftly, with top officials determined to uncover the truth. After a thorough month-long probe, it was revealed that several officers had indeed abused their power. They had illegally accessed and provided Ahsan's location details to Fazil Hussain. The responsible officers were promptly suspended, their actions condemned as a betrayal of public trust.

Amidst the tension, Fazil Hussain's family thought it prudent to marry off Varda immediately, opting to hold the wedding a night before the originally planned date. This rushed decision was driven by the fear of further scandal and the hope that a quick marriage might deflect some of the mounting criticism.

Fazil Hussain, realizing the gravity of the situation, sought to mitigate the damage. He sent messages to Faraz Khan through intermediaries, expressing his deepest apologies and seeking forgiveness. Fazil pleaded with Faraz not to proceed with the police case against them for abetment of suicide. In a bid to demonstrate his sincerity, he even offered to return the money he had taken from Faraz, hoping this gesture might soften the animosity between the families.

The once-powerful Fazil Hussain now found himself in a desperate position, trying to salvage what little remained of his family's reputation. The entire ordeal had left an indelible mark on Kushalgram, a reminder of how quickly the tides of public opinion can turn when the truth is unveiled.

Faraz Khan and his family were distraught. The house, once filled with the usual hustle and bustle, now echoed with an eerie silence. Ahsan's mother, in particular, had withdrawn into herself. She sat in one corner, eyes vacant, staring blankly at something far off. The relatives, concerned and compassionate, tried everything to make her cry, believing that shedding tears might bring her some relief. They spoke softly to her, held her hands, and even recounted memories of Ahsan. But nothing seemed to break her trance. Her eyes remained dry, devoid of any trace of tears, as if the well of her sorrow had run too deep to overflow.

Faraz, though equally heartbroken, took it upon himself to manage the affairs of the household. He moved about with a heavy heart, trying to console his sons and daughters who were equally shaken. The brothers, already harbouring a simmering anger towards Ahsan for his perceived recklessness, were now also burdened with guilt and sorrow. They regretted their harshness, but the weight of the scandal and their mother's condition left them feeling helpless and lost.

In the midst of this emotional turmoil, the inquiry and its outcomes brought no solace. The suspension of officers who had misused their power to track Ahsan's location seemed a hollow victory. The damage was done, and the void left by Ahsan's supposed suicide was too profound to be filled by mere justice.

As the day turned to night, the atmosphere grew even heavier. Ahsan's mother remained in her corner, a silent testament to the depth of her grief. Faraz tried to encourage her to eat, to rest, to speak, but she remained unresponsive. Her silence spoke volumes, a heartbreaking reminder of the pain that words could not express.

The rest of the family, trying to cope with their own grief, kept a constant vigil over her, hoping for a sign, a word, anything that might indicate she was still with them in spirit. But for now, all they could do was wait and hope that time might bring some semblance of healing to their shattered hearts.

Then came the most difficult part. Ahsan's brothers travelled to Kolkata, hoping to get more information about their brother and, more painstakingly, to find and bring his mortal remains back home. Everyone was praying for a miracle, holding onto a slim hope that maybe somehow, someone had saved Ahsan from drowning.

Upon reaching Kolkata, they immediately filed a police complaint and showed them the video. The police identified the spot as the Vidyasagar Bridge and confirmed that the video, the bridge, and the phone call stating that a young man had jumped from the bridge matched the description and circumstances surrounding Ahsan's disappearance.

The authorities began a thorough search operation in the river, but hope was dwindling with each passing hour. As the search continued, a call came in for Ahsan's eldest brother from the hotel where Ahsan had stayed. The hotel manager informed them that it had been three days since Ahsan had not returned to his room. Concerned, the management had opened the room and found all his belongings neatly packed. They also discovered another suicide note, written and signed by Ahsan.

In this second note, Ahsan reiterated his allegations against Fazil Hussain, Varda, the corrupt policemen, and the three contract killers, holding them responsible for his suicide. He also made a final request, asking the hotel management to kindly contact his elder brother to come down and gather his belongings and take them back to his mother.

The brothers, overwhelmed with grief, collected Ahsan's belongings from the hotel. Each item they packed felt like a dagger to their hearts, a poignant reminder of their lost brother. The suicide note was a devastating confirmation of the torment Ahsan had endured. They could feel the weight of his suffering in every word he wrote.

Returning to the police station with the new evidence, they hoped it would strengthen their case against Fazil Hussain and the others implicated in Ahsan's notes. The search for Ahsan's body continued, but the discovery of the note shifted the focus, adding another layer to the investigation.

Back home, the family awaited any news with bated breath. Ahsan's mother, still silent and withdrawn, seemed to sense the gravity of the situation through the whispers and solemn faces around her. The return of Ahsan's brothers with his belongings and the note was a moment of profound sorrow. They handed the note to their father, who read it with trembling hands, his eyes welling up with tears.

The family, once united in joy and strength, now stood fractured by grief and the weight of unanswered questions. The pain of their loss was compounded by the knowledge that their son and brother had suffered deeply, his last days marked by betrayal and despair.

Chapter 11

Faraz Khan decreed that he would not proceed further with the police case against Fazil Hussain and his daughter, provided they leave Kushalgram forever. He wanted to close this chapter once and for all, seeking to prevent further pain and heartache for his family. Pursuing the police proceedings would mean keeping the wound open, reliving the trauma day after day, which he simply did not have the strength to endure.

The amount of money taken by Fazil Hussain was returned, but neither Faraz nor his family touched it. Instead, they decided to donate the entire sum to charity in Ahsan's name. This act of charity was a way to honour Ahsan's memory, turning their pain into a gesture of goodwill that would benefit others, even as they struggled with their own grief.

The family hoped that by severing ties with Fazil Hussain and his daughter and by channelling the money into something positive, they could begin to heal. It was a small step towards finding peace in the wake of such a profound loss.

As news of their decision spread through Kushalgram, the townspeople saw it as an act of grace and strength. Many admired the Khan family for their ability to rise above vengeance and bitterness, even in their darkest hour. The charity established in Ahsan's name became a symbol of hope and a testament to his family's enduring love and integrity.

While the pain of Ahsan's loss would never fully disappear, Faraz Khan's decree allowed the family to start the long process of healing. They knew it would take time, but they held onto the belief that one day, the memories of Ahsan would bring more smiles than tears, and his legacy would be one of compassion and strength.

Part 2

Chapter 12

Six Months Later, Mumbai

Dinesh Bhai Patel, fondly known as Dinu Kaka, was a man in his late sixties, and he ran a modest courier office at Crawford Market, Mumbai. Two side by side shops were occupied by Dinesh Bhai on the ground floor of a commercial complex. The first shop was dedicated to the courier business, while the next shop with just a non-descript door in between that led into the inner office where the real action happened. The next shop, though simple, was equipped with essential tools for the hawala business.

Here, Dinu Kaka and Ihfaaz conducted their operations. The room housed a computer, a printer, a shredding machine, a note-counting machine, and a modest stash of cash. Additionally, there were 4 to 5 telephones and 3 to 4 mobile phones scattered around, reflecting the scale and complexity of their operations. Despite its unassuming appearance, the hawala office was the hub of their financial transactions, away from the prying eyes of the outside world and totally non connected to the courier office.

As Dinu Kaka prepared for lunch, he called out to Ihfaaz, inviting him to join. Ihfaaz, however, asked him to go ahead as he was engrossed in pending work. Dinu Kaka, with his usual warmth, lovingly scolded him to take care of himself, sharing a Gujarati proverb: "Business always stays young; it is the businessmen who grow old." Despite this, Ihfaaz's appearance remained unchanged—a faint smile that rarely broke through his usual focus and profound sadness.

Ihfaaz's smile was brief, almost imperceptible, before he returned to his work. For the past five months, Dinu Kaka had come to understand the depths of Ihfaaz's sadness. The young man's eyes held a constant shadow, a profound sadness that no amount of jovial conversation seemed to dispel. Ihfaaz was always focused, his face serious and preoccupied, as though the weight of unseen burdens bore down on him.

As Dinu Kaka walked out the door, his steps echoing in the quiet office, he glanced back at Ihfaaz. Despite the youthful appearance and earnest dedication, the young man's aura was one of heavy contemplation. Dinu Kaka hoped that one day, Ihfaaz would find a reason to lift the veil of sorrow that seemed to follow him. For now, he contented himself with small victories—the rare moments when Ihfaaz's lips would curve into a smile, however fleeting.

The hustle and bustle of Mumbai continued outside, indifferent to the lives it intersected. Yet within the confines of the courier office, a different story unfolded—one of silent struggles and unspoken sorrows. Dinu Kaka's thoughts lingered on Ihfaaz as he made his way to lunch, wishing for a brighter future for the young man who had become like family to him.

As Dinu Kaka left for lunch, Ihfaaz turned his attention to the pending work at hand. But suddenly, his reflection on the glass partition caught his attention. The journey from Ahsan to Ihfaaz had made him unrecognizable. Gone were the long and fashionable hair, replaced with a military crew cut. The lean body had been transformed into a muscular tone, thanks to the hours spent at the gym. The stubble was replaced with a clean-shaven look. The most striking change was in his eyes and face. Earlier, his eyes used to be lively and always had a mischievous twinkle in them; now, they dispelled a steely resolve and a strange emptiness. The face that once radiated happiness and carried a smile was now replaced with a serious appearance.

He stared at himself for a moment, contemplating the transformation. The path he had chosen was not an easy one, but it was necessary. Every change he had made, every step he had taken, was a means to an end. Ihfaaz knew that the journey ahead was fraught with challenges, but his determination to see it through kept him going. The reflection in the glass served as a reminder of the price he had paid and the purpose that now drove him.

Chapter 13

Ihfaaz's gaze remained fixed on his reflection, but his thoughts began to drift back six months to that fateful conversation with his mother. The memory was vivid, replaying in his mind like a haunting echo. After stepping out of the shower that night, with the cold water washing away his despair, he had emerged with a steely resolve. There was no sense in crying over the past; what was done was done. The only way forward was to gather himself up and ensure that he exacted revenge on everyone who had wronged him.

Varda, the main culprit, would be the first. Her betrayal had shattered his world, and for that, she would pay dearly. Her father, who had extorted money from his family and even sent contract killers after him, was next on his list. And then, there were his brothers—those who should have stood by him during the darkest phase of his life but instead chose to be indifferent. Their lack of support stung just as deeply as the betrayal from outsiders.

Sitting deep in thought, Ihfaaz began to methodically plan his course of action. Each wrong, each betrayal, would be avenged. The more he thought, the clearer his path became. Finally, he moved to his writing table, where he meticulously wrote down each and everything that needed to be done. Every detail, every step, was outlined with precision. His resolve was unshakable, his purpose clear.

There would be no mercy, no hesitation. Ihfaaz was no longer the man who once loved and trusted blindly. He was now driven by a singular focus: revenge. And he would stop at nothing until justice, as he saw it, was served.

First and foremost, Ihfaaz knew that he needed a new identity—one that would symbolize his transformation and shield him from the past.

The name "Ahsan" no longer fit; it belonged to a man who had been betrayed and broken. He decided to rename himself Ihfaaz, a name that meant "the protector" or "the protected one." It was a name that would reflect his new purpose and the armour he was building around his heart.

Secondly, he realized that staying in Kolkata was out of the question. The city held too many memories, too many ties to a life he was leaving behind. He needed a place where he could blend in, where the ghosts of his past wouldn't follow. After careful consideration, he zeroed in on Mumbai. The bustling metropolis, with its endless sea of people, offered the perfect anonymity. In Mumbai, he could disappear into the crowd, laying the groundwork for his plans without attracting attention.

Then came the tricky part: making sure his disappearance was flawless. Ahsan knew that if he executed his plan perfectly, his vanishing act would create chaos for Varda and her family, throwing them into a spiral of confusion and panic. The first step was to create the illusion of his suicide while ensuring his new life was ready to begin seamlessly.

He checked into another hotel while still keeping his current room. The new room became his staging ground, where he gathered all the essentials for his new identity—a fresh set of clothes, a new laptop, new footwear, and everything else he would need to start over. His existing belongings—his clothes, laptop, and personal items—would be left in the old room for his brothers to collect, along with the carefully crafted suicide note he planned to leave behind. It would be the perfect setup to convince them that he was gone for good.

All of this required money, which he obtained by messaging his brother, fabricating a story about being hospitalized and needing funds. The deception worked, and the money was transferred to him without question. With the funds secured, Ihfaaz booked a night train ticket to Mumbai, choosing the day when he would record the video announcing his supposed suicide. He deliberately booked himself in First AC to limit his interactions with other passengers, ensuring that he remained as unnoticed as possible during the journey. Flying was out of the question, as it would leave a paper trail—a risk he couldn't afford to take.

One crucial decision still loomed: where to procure the papers for his new identity. Should he arrange them in Kolkata or wait until he reached Mumbai? After much thought, Ihfaaz decided that his new identity would be born in Mumbai. The city was vast, impersonal, and perfect for someone looking to start over without a trace. There, he could blend into the background, and the new life of Ihfaaz would truly begin.

Chapter 14

On the day before Varda's wedding, Ahsan meticulously went through his room, scanning every corner to ensure he hadn't left behind anything that could hint at his true intentions. His heart raced as he checked and double-checked, but to his relief, the room was immaculate—nothing was out of place, and nothing remained that could betray his plan.

Satisfied that everything was in order, he took one last look around the room before quietly slipping out. The time had come for the next phase of his plan. He made his way through the city, heading towards Vidyasagar Bridge, the chosen location for the final act of his deception.

The bridge, with its towering structure and the steady flow of traffic beneath it, was the perfect place to stage the conclusion of Ahsan's story and the beginning of Ihfaaz's. He stood there for a moment, taking in the view, and then steeled himself for what was to come. The world would soon believe that Ahsan Faraz Khan had ended his life, and the man known as Ihfaaz would disappear into the night, leaving nothing behind but questions, chaos, and a haunting legacy for those who had wronged him.

After calling the emergency police number from the phone booth and informing them of his own suicide, Ahsan took a taxi to his new hotel room near Howrah station. Upon arriving, he gathered all his belongings, carefully checking to ensure nothing was left behind. After checking out, he treated himself to a quiet dinner, savouring the solitude and finality of his actions.

With his resolve unshaken, he then headed to Howrah station to board the train that would take him to Mumbai and a new life. As the train rumbled into the station, the weight of his past began to lift. Ahsan Faraz Khan was no more. From now on, there was only Ihfaaz, and the road ahead was his to carve out—filled with the promise of revenge, transformation, and a future forged in the fires of betrayal.

In his initial days in Mumbai, Ihfaaz had planned to leverage his computer skills to find a job and integrate himself into the city's fabric. Despite having ample cash, he knew that he needed a steady source of income to sustain himself over the long term. Each morning, he would rise early to explore the area around his hotel, studying the neighbourhood and familiarizing himself with his new surroundings. He kept an eye on the newspapers for any job openings, and after lunch, he would head to an upscale café to enjoy coffee and use their free Wi-Fi.

One day, as Ihfaaz was leaving the hotel, he noticed Dinu Kaka struggling to open the shutter of his office. His regular staff had not yet arrived, and the elderly man seemed to be having a hard time managing it alone. Seeing an opportunity to help, Ihfaaz approached and offered assistance. Dinu Kaka was grateful and thanked him profusely. He insisted that Ihfaaz join him for a cup of tea as a gesture of thanks.

This act of kindness sparked the beginning of their acquaintance. Over the next 8 to 10 days, Ihfaaz and Dinu Kaka developed a routine of sharing tea, which provided Ihfaaz with valuable insights into the local area and a sense of camaraderie.

Eventually, Dinu Kaka inquired about Ihfaaz's background. Ihfaaz crafted a fabricated story to explain his presence in Mumbai. He claimed that he had been unable to complete his graduation due to family problems. His tale was that his family had faced significant issues, leaving him with no immediate relatives alive. The only family member he mentioned was a distant grandmother, who was too frail and unwell to support him. This story was designed to explain his situation while keeping his true identity and motives concealed.

Ihfaaz's fabricated past was carefully constructed to provide just enough detail to seem plausible while avoiding any deeper scrutiny. It allowed him to blend into his new surroundings and gain Dinu Kaka's trust, a crucial step in his plan to establish himself in Mumbai.

Chapter 15

During one of their regular tea meetings, Ihfaaz casually mentioned to Dinu Kaka that he was looking for a job. Without hesitation, Dinu Kaka offered him a position in his office. He explained that his only son had no interest in the family business, leaving him severely short-handed. With Ihfaaz's educational background, Dinu Kaka believed he would be the perfect fit to help manage the operations.

Ihfaaz asked for a day to consider the offer, and after weighing his options, he decided to accept it. The next day, he joined DP Logistics and Courier as a manager, marking the official start of his new life in Mumbai. This position not only provided him with a steady income but also gave him a sense of purpose as he continued to navigate his new identity and plan for the future.

Ihfaaz's swift transformation of DP Logistics and Courier impressed Dinu Kaka immensely. Within just a month, Ihfaaz's innovations were already paying off. The switch from manual entries to computerized systems streamlined operations, reducing errors and improving efficiency. His most significant change was the strategic separation of the courier and hawala businesses into two distinct shops. By doing so, he minimized the risk of drawing unwanted attention to their more sensitive operations, ensuring that the businesses appeared unrelated to any outsiders. This move not only safeguarded the hawala operations but also enhanced the overall reputation of DP Logistics and Courier.

Within three months of joining DP Logistics and Courier, Ihfaaz had taken full control of the hawala operation, impressing Dinu Kaka with his efficiency and modern approach. The once-cluttered office, filled with old-school registers and ledgers, was now a streamlined, computerized system. Ihfaaz had meticulously digitized every aspect of the business, ensuring that all transactions were handled online, significantly reducing the risk of errors and improving the overall speed and accuracy of the operations.

Dinu Kaka, recognizing the immense value Ihfaaz brought to the business, decided to make his life a little easier. He persuaded Ihfaaz to move out of the small, nondescript hotel room he had been staying in since arriving in Mumbai. Dinu Kaka found a modest 1 BHK flat nearby and fronted the advance deposit for the apartment. He also assured Ihfaaz that he would take care of the monthly rent, a gesture that spoke volumes about his trust in the young man.

Ihfaaz, in turn, repaid this trust with unwavering dedication. He approached his work with a level of focus and precision that was rare. He would arrive at the office before anyone else, carefully reviewing the previous day's transactions and ensuring everything was in order. His attention to detail was unmatched, and he was always one step ahead, anticipating potential issues and resolving them before they could escalate.

In the past six months, Ihfaaz had managed to establish himself in Mumbai, creating proper identity documents under his new name. His life had settled into a routine that allowed him to blend seamlessly into the bustling city. Everything seemed to be going smoothly, but a lingering frustration gnawed at him—despite his meticulous planning and efforts, he had yet to take the first step toward the ultimate goal he had set for himself when he left Kolkata. Yet, Ihfaaz remained patient, believing that destiny was on his side and that, at the right moment, he would receive the guidance he needed.

It must have been around 15 to 20 minutes since Dinu Kaka had left for lunch when Ihfaaz was jolted out of his thoughts. A knock on the door broke his concentration, and before he could fully comprehend what was happening, four to five policemen entered the office, followed closely by a police inspector. The sudden intrusion sent a surge of adrenaline through Ihfaaz, his mind racing as he tried to assess the situation.

Shahana's Story.

Shahana Faraz Khan was a woman of remarkable strength and resilience, a figure of quiet yet unwavering support in the Khan household. Born into a modest family, she had always been pragmatic and sharp-minded, qualities that served her well throughout her life. When she married Faraz Khan, a man of ambition and dreams far beyond his humble beginnings, Shahana knew that her life would be anything but ordinary.

Together, they embarked on a journey from a life of mediocrity to one of considerable wealth and influence. Faraz was driven, his focus on building a business empire that would secure their future and establish the Khan family as a formidable name in their community. Shahana, for her part, was the anchor that kept everything grounded. She never questioned the morality of her husband's business dealings; her loyalty and trust in Faraz were absolute. In her eyes, her duty was to stand by him, offering her support as he navigated the complex and often treacherous world of business.

As Faraz Khan poured his energy into expanding his business, Shahana took on the dual role of mother and father to their children. She was the steady presence in their lives, providing them with the guidance, discipline, and love they needed. She managed the household with efficiency and grace, ensuring that despite Faraz's long absences, their children never felt neglected. Her strong will and intelligence shone through in the way she handled every challenge that came her way, whether it was a financial setback or a family crisis.

Faraz respected her deeply for this. He knew that without Shahana's strength and support, he would never have been able to achieve the success he had. Their relationship was built on mutual respect and a deep, unspoken understanding of their roles. While Faraz was the face of the family's public success, Shahana was its backbone, the one who kept everything from falling apart.

Shahana's life was not without its trials. The journey from modest beginnings to wealth was fraught with difficulties, but she faced each one with determination. She remained stoic in the face of adversity, whether it was financial struggles in the early days or the challenges that came with raising their children. Her sacrifices were many, but she never wavered, believing that her role in supporting her husband and raising their children was her true calling.

In her heart, Shahana harboured a deep love for her family. Her children were her pride, and despite the demands of managing the household and supporting Faraz, she always made time for them. She instilled in them the values of hard work, integrity, and loyalty—values that she held dear.

When the crisis surrounding Ahsan unfolded, Shahana instinctively trusted her son, believing in the values she had instilled in him over the years. She stood by him with unwavering support, an action that many, including her own family, mistook as mere maternal bias toward her youngest child. However, Shahana's loyalty was rooted not just in love but in a deep conviction that Ahsan was being wronged.

What surprised her most was the stark difference in how her elder sons reacted. They quickly distanced themselves from Ahsan, blaming him for the family's turmoil without ever pausing to consider his side of the story. Their coldness was a betrayal that Shahana had never anticipated. But what truly bewildered her was her husband's alignment with their elder sons, siding against Ahsan without question.

Despite all her feelings, Shahana knew it wouldn't be right to maintain secret contact with her son. So, with a heavy heart, she refrained from answering his calls. Ahsan had developed a routine of giving her missed calls at various times of the day, and she was relieved each time she saw those missed calls, knowing at least that he was alive and well.

However, when Ahsan fell ill and couldn't call, her worry grew. Ignoring her husband's directive, she called his number repeatedly, but each attempt went unanswered. She spent a sleepless night, consumed by fear that something terrible had happened to her son. When he finally answered her call the next morning, she heaved a deep sigh of relief. From that point on, they began calling each other regularly in secret, sharing moments of solace without the rest of the family knowing.

On the day before his planned suicide, Ahsan called his mother, his voice low and filled with urgency. Shahana, sensing something was amiss, listened carefully as he asked her for a favour, but before he could say anything further, he insisted on one condition.

"Ammi, promise me that whatever I tell you now, you will not share it with anyone," Ahsan said, his tone almost pleading.

Shahana hesitated for a moment. "Ahsan, what is this about? You're scaring me. What are you planning?"

"Please, Ammi, just promise me," Ahsan repeated, his voice trembling slightly.

After a long pause, Shahana finally agreed. "Alright, Ahsan, I promise. But tell me, what's going on?"

Ahsan took a deep breath before he began to outline his plan. "Ammi, I've thought about this long and hard. The only way to clear my name, to protect our family, is if I disappear... if everyone thinks I'm dead."

As Shahana listened to Ahsan's plan, a wave of dread washed over her. She couldn't believe what she was hearing. Her son, her youngest, was talking about faking his own death. The idea was so extreme, so final, that it made her heart ache.

"Ahsan, this is madness," Shahana said, her voice trembling. "You can't be serious. There has to be another way. We can fight this together, find a lawyer, talk to people—anything but this."

"Ammi, you don't understand," Ahsan replied, his tone firm yet filled with sadness. "There's no other way out. If I stay, they'll destroy me, and they'll drag our family down with them. I can't let that happen. This is the only way to protect everyone."

"But disappearing, pretending to be dead? Ahsan, that's so... so final," Shahana protested, her voice breaking. "How will you live? What kind of life will you have? Always hiding, always looking over your shoulder?"

Ahsan sighed deeply. "I know it won't be easy, Ammi. But at least I'll be alive. I'll be able to start over, to build something new. And I'll have the peace of knowing that you, Baba, and my brothers are safe."

Shahana shook her head, tears streaming down her face. "This isn't the life I wanted for you, Ahsan. I wanted you to be happy, to have a family of your own, to live a good life. And now you're asking me to accept this... this nightmare."

"I know, Ammi, I know," Ahsan said, his voice filled with pain. "But I don't have a choice. If I stay, they'll never stop coming after me. And they'll hurt all of you to get to me. I can't live with that on my conscience."

Shahana was silent for a moment, trying to gather her thoughts. "Ahsan, please, just think about it some more. There has to be another way. We can find a way to fight them, to expose their lies. You're innocent, Ahsan. We can prove it."

Ahsan's voice softened as he responded. "Ammi, I've thought about this for a long time. I've weighed every option, and this is the only way. It's not just about proving my innocence anymore; it's about keeping all of you safe. If I disappear, they'll have nothing left to use against us. And eventually, the truth will come out."

"But Ahsan," Shahana pleaded, "what if something goes wrong? What if you get caught? What if you can't come back? I can't bear the thought of losing you like this."

"Ammi," Ahsan said gently, "nothing is without risk. But I've planned this carefully. I know what I'm doing. And I promise you, I'll be okay. I'll keep in touch, and one day, when the time is right, I'll come back."

Shahana's heart ached with every word he spoke. She wanted to believe him, to trust that he knew what he was doing, but the fear of losing her son was overwhelming. "Ahsan, please... don't do this. We can face this together. We're a family. We can fight this."

Ahsan's voice was firm but filled with love. "We are a family, Ammi. And that's why I have to do this. To protect you, to protect everyone. I'm not giving up; I'm just... changing the plan. And I need you to trust me."

Shahana felt a deep sense of helplessness, knowing that her words were not enough to change his mind. She wanted to keep him close, to shield him from the world, but she also knew that Ahsan was determined to go through with his plan. With a heavy heart, she realized that all she could do now was support him.

"I don't like this, Ahsan," Shahana whispered, her voice filled with sorrow. "But I trust you. Just promise me you'll stay safe, and that you'll come back to me when this is all over."

"I promise, Ammi," Ahsan said, his voice choked with emotion. "I'll come back. And when I do, we'll be together again, just like before."

Shahana held the phone tightly, wishing she could hold her son instead. "I love you, Ahsan. More than anything in this world. Don't forget that."

"I love you too, Ammi," Ahsan replied, his voice filled with warmth. "And I'll always carry that love with me, no matter where I am."

As they ended the call, Shahana sat in silence, her heart heavy with the knowledge of what was to come. She had made her promise, but the pain of what it meant was almost too much to bear. She prayed for her son's safety, hoping that somehow, against all odds, they would find their way back to each other.

Now, all Shahana could do was await the drama to unfold. Her family didn't suspect anything, as her sadness had been evident since the events surrounding Ahsan began. She maintained a stoic silence, her eyes heavy with an unspoken sorrow. So, when the news of Ahsan's purported suicide finally broke, she simply sat motionless, silently praying for her son's well-being.

People around her tried to console her, urging her to cry, to release the pain they assumed she was holding in. But Shahana didn't respond. How was she supposed to cry over the death of her son when she knew, in her heart, that he was still alive? The irony of the situation gnawed at her—how much more cruel could fate be, forcing her to mourn a son who had only just stepped into a new life?

The days following the news passed in a blur. Shahana performed the rituals, accepted condolences, and wore the mask of a grieving mother. But inside, she was waiting, yearning for a sign, a hint that her son had successfully escaped into the life they had secretly planned.

It was on the third day after the news broke that she received a missed call from an unknown number. Her heart skipped a beat as she saw it, and she quickly pocketed her phone, waiting for the right moment. When she was certain that she was alone, she dialed the number back, her hands trembling slightly.

The phone rang just once before a familiar voice answered on the other end. "Assalamoalaikum Ammi, myself Ihfaaz Ahmed Khan speaking."

Shahana's heart pounded in her chest, the voice was unmistakable, yet there was something profoundly different about it. The conversation that followed was a blur of emotions and reassurances, but one thing stood out clearly: the finality in Ahsan's tone.

As he spoke, his voice was steady and resolute, a marked departure from the Ahsan she had known. The change in name wasn't just a new identity; it was a declaration of his complete break from the past. The way he addressed her, the formality in his speech, and the determination underlying his words all spoke volumes.

As their conversation ended, the sense of closure was bittersweet. While she was relieved to hear his voice and know he was alive, the realization that he had embarked on a path with such finality filled her with a deep, lingering sadness. Her son, now Ihfaaz, had made his choice and committed to a course that meant he was no longer the Ahsan she had known.

Chapter 16

Hawala is an informal and ancient system of money transfer that operates outside the bounds of the legal banking system. It is predominantly used by individuals who want to transfer money without leaving a trace that could be recorded by banks or monitored by government agencies. The entire system hinges on the trust established between hawala agents across different locations.

A person wishing to send money would approach a local hawala agent, hand over the cash, and provide the details of the recipient. The agent would then contact a counterpart in the recipient's location. The recipient would receive the money, usually within a day or two, without any formal documentation or involvement of banks. The agent charges a fee for this service.

The unique aspect of hawala is that physical money rarely needs to be moved between locations. Instead, the hawala agents maintain detailed ledgers of all transactions. These ledgers allow them to balance out the money owed between them over time. On rare occasions, when a physical transfer of cash is necessary to settle accounts, they may use the infrastructure of a courier company to discreetly move the money.

This system is widely used due to its efficiency, low cost, and the secrecy it offers. However, because it operates outside of the formal economy, it is often associated with illegal activities such as money laundering and financing terrorism, making it a target for law enforcement agencies.

Despite being involved in the illegal Hawala business, Dinu Kaka's operation wasn't large enough to attract much attention from law enforcement. His business had always flown under the radar, and on that fateful day, he was away for lunch when the police decided to raid his office.

As soon as the police burst through the door, Ihfaaz, who had been seated at his desk, immediately sensed the gravity of the situation. His mind raced, but his training in IT and the foresight he had always maintained for such a scenario kicked in. With the police officers distracted by the sudden entry, Ihfaaz discreetly pressed a combination of keys on his computer. In a matter of seconds, the entire data on the system was encrypted—a protective measure he had designed long before this day.

The significance of this action was monumental. Had the office still operated on the old-school manual accounting system, all the incriminating evidence would have been laid bare for the police to seize. But with the data now securely encrypted, there was no immediate evidence available for the officers to use against them.

The police, unaware of Ihfaaz's swift action, focused on other aspects of the raid. They seized all the cash and computers present in the office and arrested Ihfaaz for his involvement in the illegal Hawala operation. The office was promptly sealed, marking it as a crime scene. However, in the chaos, the non-descript courier office adjacent to the Hawala operation was left untouched, thanks to Ihfaaz's prudence in separating the two businesses earlier.

As the commotion unfolded, Dinu Kaka returned from lunch and saw the police swarming his office. Panic threatened to take over, but before he could act rashly, Ihfaaz discreetly signalled him to stay away. Understanding the silent communication, Dinu Kaka made the tough decision to leave the premises immediately. Though he was deeply concerned for Ihfaaz's well-being, he knew the best course of action was to contact his lawyer and prepare for the next steps.

Ihfaaz was taken to the police station, leaving Dinu Kaka to contemplate the implications of the raid. The sealed Hawala office was a significant blow, but the courier office remained operational, a lifeline that Ihfaaz's foresight had preserved. Dinu Kaka couldn't help but feel a deep sense of gratitude towards Ihfaaz, who had risked everything to protect the business.

The raid had gone down just as quickly as it had begun, leaving the office in shambles and Ihfaaz in custody. Dinu Kaka's lawyer arrived at the police station almost immediately after hearing the news, a man known for his connections and ability to navigate the murky waters of legal troubles. He was determined to get Ihfaaz out, utilizing every trick in the book. Offering bribes, proposing a personal bail bond—nothing was off the table.

But the officer in charge, Giriraj Patil, was not one to be swayed easily. His reputation as a strict and upright officer preceded him, and with the amount of evidence collected, he was in no mood to let Ihfaaz walk free. Patil flatly refused all offers, his stern expression leaving no room for negotiation.

"Take it to the court," Patil told the lawyer with finality. "Seek bail when we present him tomorrow. Until then, he stays here."

The lawyer had no choice but to comply, though he wasn't pleased. It was clear that Ihfaaz would spend at least the entire day and night in the police lockup, a reality that was slowly sinking in as he was led away to his cell. The cold, hard truth of his situation began to weigh on him, but Ihfaaz knew this was just another challenge to overcome.

Despite the gravity of his predicament, Ihfaaz remained calm. He had done what he could to protect the business, and more importantly, Dinu Kaka. The data was encrypted, the courier office untouched, and the most crucial evidence safely hidden. All that remained was to endure what was to come next.

As he sat in the lockup, the gravity of the situation set in. The room was dimly lit, the air thick with a mix of stale sweat and fear. The faint sound of distant conversations and the clanking of metal bars echoed through the corridor. Ihfaaz settled into a corner, his thoughts racing but his expression calm. He had played his part well, and now, he had to face the consequences of his actions.

Meanwhile, Dinu Kaka, though anxious, knew that Ihfaaz had done everything possible to protect them. The lawyer, though unsuccessful in securing his immediate release, would be back in court the next day to argue for bail. Until then, they had to wait and hope for the best.

The evening brought an unexpected visit from Dinu Kaka's lawyer, who had come to deliver food and gather signatures for some legal documents. As the lawyer entered the dimly lit lockup, he was startled to see Ihfaaz in a dire state—wearing only his pants, his body bore the signs of a severe beating, and his face looked pale and exhausted.

The lawyer, trying to mask his shock, inquired softly, "What happened, Ihfaaz? You look terrible."

Ihfaaz, his voice strained but calm, responded, "From the afternoon until now, they've been beating me, trying to break me. They made it clear they don't care about charging me. All they want is for me to turn over Dinesh Patel, to become a state approver and give evidence against him."

The lawyer clenched his jaw, understanding the gravity of the situation. "And you refused?"

"Of course, I did," Ihfaaz replied, his resolve unshaken. "That's why I'm in this state. This Inspector, Giriraj Patil, seems to have some personal grudge against Dinu Kaka, or maybe he's been bribed to frame him. Patil's actions are too aggressive for a routine case."

The lawyer nodded, deep in thought. "You're right. Patil's reputation is that of a straightforward officer, but he's not one to act without reason. There must be something more behind this."

"That's what I need you to find out," Ihfaaz said, leaning closer despite the pain in his body. "Focus all your efforts on uncovering why

Patil is pushing this so hard. Only then can we figure out how to get me out of here. Because right now, it doesn't look like I'll be getting bail tomorrow."

The lawyer's expression hardened with determination. "I'll do everything I can, Ihfaaz. We'll get to the bottom of this."

As the lawyer left, Ihfaaz steeled himself for the night ahead. He knew the torture would continue, but he was prepared to endure it. His mind was focused on the bigger picture, on the strategy that would eventually set him free. He was determined not to betray Dinu Kaka, no matter the cost.

The night was a gruelling test of endurance. Ihfaaz could feel every minute stretch into eternity as he withstood the relentless interrogation. It was a battle of wills—who would tire first, Ihfaaz or the constables under Giriraj Patil's command. The hours crawled by, and just when Ihfaaz thought the ordeal would never end, he noticed a shift in the room's energy. It was past 2 AM, and finally, Giriraj Patil decided to call it a night. The inspector, seeing that Ihfaaz hadn't cracked, concluded that it was just a matter of time. If not tonight, then in the next couple of days, Ihfaaz would surely break—or so Patil thought.

The next morning, as the sun crept over the horizon, Ihfaaz was dragged out of his cell, still bruised and battered from the night's events, and taken to court. His lawyer met him there, the concern evident in his eyes as he saw Ihfaaz's condition. They were granted a brief private conversation, just ten minutes before the hearing began.

"Ihfaaz, I've got some crucial information," the lawyer began, his voice low and urgent. "I think I've figured out why Patil is so hell-bent on breaking you and going after Dinu Kaka."

Ihfaaz, despite his physical exhaustion, leaned in, his interest piqued. "What is it?"

"Patil's son is studying in an engineering college in Pune. Recently, there was a birthday party at one of his friend's hostel room, which the college authorities raided. They found alcohol in the room. All the students at the party were rusticated, pending an investigation. It's serious—those found guilty could be expelled, and worse, blacklisted from joining any other college or university for the foreseeable future. Patil's son was among them."

Ihfaaz narrowed his eyes, sensing where this was going. "So, Patil's trying to keep this under wraps?"

"Exactly. The college hasn't involved the police yet, fearing the scandal it could create. But there's strong reason to believe that Patil is trying to gather as much cash as possible, likely to bribe the disciplinary committee to get his son out of this mess. That's why he's coming down so hard on you and Dinu Kaka—he needs the money, and he's willing to do whatever it takes to get it."

Despite the strong arguments presented by his lawyer, Ihfaaz's bid for bail was denied. The court's decision meant that he would face another gruelling day in police custody. The relentless interrogation and harsh treatment continued as Inspector Giriraj Patil walked into Ihfaaz's cell with a renewed sense of urgency.

"Enough of this charade, Ihfaaz," Patil said, his tone cold and authoritative. "Just give me Dinesh Patel. It'll be easier for both of us."

Ihfaaz met Patil's gaze squarely, his eyes unflinching despite the bruises and exhaustion. For a fleeting moment, Patil was taken aback by the intensity of Ihfaaz's stare.

"Sir," Ihfaaz began, his voice steady despite the pain, "beating me, torturing me, or locking up Dinu Kaka won't help clear your son's name. The truth is, your son's situation is far more complicated."

Patil's face contorted with a mixture of rage and disbelief. Without a second thought, he slapped Ihfaaz hard across the face. The force of the slap made Ihfaaz stumble to the ground. The sharp sting of the blow was not just physical but also a testament to the escalating tension. The slap left a visible mark on Ihfaaz's face, and Patil knew this act would likely become an issue in court the following day.

But Ihfaaz quickly regained his footing and stood tall, his expression betraying no sign of the pain he felt. "Sir, we need to work together to help your son out. I'm sure he's innocent and just happened to be in the wrong place at the wrong time."

Patil, now momentarily stunned by Ihfaaz's resilience and the suggestion of collaboration, took a step back. Despite knowing that Ihfaaz was merely an employee in Dinu Kaka's office, Patil couldn't ignore the courage and determination of the young man before him. Ihfaaz had endured relentless torture yet still managed to hold on to his composure and suggest a path forward.

Patil, grappling with the hopelessness of his situation, realized that no amount of money or middlemen's assurances would clear his son's name. The gravity of the situation weighed heavily on him, and for the first time, he considered that perhaps Ihfaaz could offer something he hadn't anticipated.

Desperation drove Patil to entertain the possibility of working with Ihfaaz. He didn't fully understand how this collaboration might unfold, but in the midst of his desperation, he saw a sliver of hope. Perhaps, just perhaps, this young man might hold the key to unravelling the mess and providing a way out.

The night after his intense confrontation with Inspector Patil, Ihfaaz found some comfort, as no one bothered him. The next day, he was granted bail. Although his lawyer assured him that the bail was granted on merit, Ihfaaz felt bound by the promise he had made to Inspector Patil.

After his release, Ihfaaz took some time to freshen up and have lunch at his flat before heading to meet Dinu Kaka at the courier office.

The hawala office was still sealed by the police, but his lawyer was confident that access would be restored within a few days.

When Ihfaaz arrived, Dinu Kaka was overwhelmed with gratitude. He couldn't understand how someone who had only known him for six months would risk everything to protect him. But Ihfaaz, staying focused, told Dinu Kaka that they would discuss this later. Right now, they had a more urgent task: finding a way to secure a clean chit for Inspector Patil's son.

Chapter 17

Ihfaaz called Inspector Patil and arranged to meet with his son that evening. They chose a discreet location to avoid drawing attention—Patil's modest, out-of-the-way apartment. As they settled into the small living room, Ihfaaz noticed the tension on his face, who seemed both anxious and defensive, as if bracing for another interrogation.

Ihfaaz began gently, wanting to ease the young man into the conversation. "I'm not here to judge or accuse," Ihfaaz assured him. "I just need to understand what happened so we can figure out the best way to help. Can you start by telling me about the party? What was the occasion?"

The young man took a deep breath, trying to calm his nerves. "It was a friend's birthday," he said. "We've known each other since the first year. Every few weeks, someone's birthday or some occasion becomes a reason to gather, relax, and forget about studies for a while. It's pretty normal around here."

"Is it normal to have alcohol at these parties?" Ihfaaz asked, his tone still even and nonjudgmental.

The young man nodded. "Yeah, it's common. Most of us are over 18, and no one really sees it as a big deal. We pool money, get some drinks, and just hang out in someone's room. It's not like we're doing anything wrong, at least not in our eyes. This was no different from any other party we've had in the hostel."

"So, how many people were at this party? And were there any newcomers or strangers this time?" Ihfaaz continued, leaning forward slightly, signalling his genuine interest.

"About twenty of us," the young man said, his brows furrowing in thought. "Mostly the usual crowd from our hostel wing. A couple of guys brought their friends along, but that's pretty standard too. The room we used is one of the bigger ones, so it's the usual spot for these gatherings. There wasn't anyone I didn't recognize."

Ihfaaz listened carefully, noting each detail. The fact that these parties were a routine and accepted by most hostel residents gave him some insight. "Were there any problems at previous parties? Any fights, complaints from other students, or warnings from the college authorities?"

The young man shook his head. "Not really. I mean, sometimes it gets loud, and the warden knocks on the door to keep it down. But nothing serious. And this time, it wasn't even that late. We were just a couple of hours into the party when the college authorities showed up."

"What did they do when they arrived?" Ihfaaz asked, sensing they were getting to the critical part of the story.

"They barged in," he said, his voice rising slightly, still upset by the memory. "They had security with them, and they started checking everyone's IDs, searching the room. When they found the alcohol, they immediately started taking pictures, making notes. They made a big deal out of it, like they'd caught us doing something much worse."

Ihfaaz tapped his fingers together thoughtfully. "You're saying these parties, with alcohol, were common, yet this time they responded as if it was an unprecedented offense. That's odd. Why target this party? Why now?"

The young man shrugged, a hint of frustration in his voice. "That's what I don't get. It's not like it was the first time, and it wasn't the biggest party either. Just a regular birthday bash. But they treated us like criminals. A lot of us got rusticated. The guy whose room it was is in bigger trouble."

Ihfaaz nodded, understanding the frustration. "Okay, we've made some progress. It's clear that this party was targeted for a reason, even if we don't know what that reason is yet. Let's take a break for tonight, get some rest. We'll meet again in the morning and see what more we can piece together. Maybe we're missing something—a clue that will tell us why this specific party was busted."

As they parted ways, Ihfaaz couldn't shake the feeling that there was more to this than met the eye. Someone had deliberately chosen to expose this party, and he needed to find out why. The answer to that question could be the key to clearing the young man's name.

The next morning, Ihfaaz met with Inspector Patil's son again, this time at a quiet café. As they sat down, Ihfaaz said, "Today, we need to focus on the disciplinary committee. You mentioned there are three members: the principal, the head of your department, and the managing trustee. Who holds the real power?"

The young man nodded, looking serious. "The principal, Dr. Mehta, is strict but usually fair. Professor Sharma, my department head, is more concerned with academics. But it's the managing trustee, Mr. Rajendra Desai, who has the final say. He's a businessman, not an educator, and everyone knows he controls the major decisions."

Ihfaaz leaned in. "What do you know about Desai? Anything that might explain why he's targeting this party?"

The young man thought for a moment. "Desai's private. He's got his hands in several businesses, and there are rumours he has political connections. He doesn't interact much with students unless it's something big."

"Desai is our key," Ihfaaz said. "We need to find out why he's interested in this case. Maybe there's a personal or financial angle. Start discreetly asking around—seniors, staff, anyone who might know about his interests or connections."

The young man agreed. "I'll talk to a professor who's been here for years. Maybe he knows something."

"Good," Ihfaaz said. "We need to understand Desai's motives. Once we know that, we can figure out how to turn this situation around."

They parted ways, each with a mission. Ihfaaz was determined to uncover Desai's motivations and help clear the young man's name, knowing this was more than just about a party—it was a game of power, and he needed to know the rules to win.

After his meeting with Inspector Patil's son, Ihfaaz knew he needed more information on Rajendra Desai, the managing trustee. He reached out to Dinu Kaka, explaining the situation and emphasizing the urgency.

Dinu Kaka nodded thoughtfully. "Desai is a powerful man. We'll need someone who knows the local scene in Pune well. I'll contact my counterpart there."

A few phone calls later, Dinu Kaka had arranged a meeting for Ihfaaz with Pradip Wakode, a shrewd operator and the go-to guy for the Pune Hawala network. Pradip had a reputation for getting things done quickly and discreetly.

The next morning, Ihfaaz travelled to Pune. He met Pradip in a small, nondescript café. Pradip was a lean man in his late thirties, with sharp eyes that missed nothing. He listened carefully as Ihfaaz laid out the details, nodding occasionally.

"So, you need dirt on Rajendra Desai, and you need it fast," Pradip summarized, leaning back in his chair. "Not an easy task, but not impossible either. Desai is involved in various businesses, and he has plenty of connections. There's bound to be something we can use."

"I know we're asking a lot, and time is short," Ihfaaz said, his voice steady. "But this is crucial. We need to find out why Desai is targeting the party and if there's any leverage we can use to sway him."

Pradip smirked. "I've handled trickier situations. Desai has a lot of skeletons in his closet, from what I've heard. Give me a couple of days. I'll dig around, see what I can find."

"Thank you, Pradip. I appreciate this," Ihfaaz replied, feeling a glimmer of hope.

Pradip stood up, extending his hand. “Consider it done. I’ll get to work immediately and keep you posted.”

As they shook hands, Ihfaaz felt a sense of relief. With Pradip’s local knowledge and resourcefulness, they had a real chance of uncovering the truth about Rajendra Desai. Time was of the essence, and Ihfaaz knew that every moment counted.

Chapter 18

It had been 15 tense days since Ihfaaz got bail. On the subsequent hearing, the police had unsealed Dinu Kaka's office, which allowed Ihfaaz to return to work. But despite resuming their regular routine, a sense of unease still hung in the air. Inspector Patil, his family, and even Ihfaaz were on edge, waiting for news from the disciplinary committee. The decision could come any day, and they all knew that everything hinged on the outcome.

It was around 6 in the evening, and Ihfaaz was sitting in Dinu Kaka's office, having tea. The quiet hum of the city outside was almost comforting. Dinu Kaka was going over some accounts, but his eyes kept flicking toward Ihfaaz, who stared blankly at his cup, lost in thought.

Suddenly, Ihfaaz's phone rang, shattering the silence. His heart leaped into his throat as he saw the caller ID—Inspector Patil's son. His hands trembled slightly as he picked up the phone, pressing it to his ear.

"Hello?" Ihfaaz said, his voice uncertain.

For a moment, he heard nothing but muffled sobs on the other end. Ihfaaz's mind raced, trying to piece together what could have happened. His concern grew with each passing second of silence.

Finally, a voice broke through the sobs. It was Inspector Patil's wife, her voice choked with emotion. "Ihfaaz, beta... may God bless you," she said between sobs. "I don't know how to thank you."

Ihfaaz's confusion deepened. "Aunty, what happened? Is everything okay?"

More sobs, then a deep breath. "It's over, beta. The committee gave my son a clean chit. They've asked him to return to college immediately!"

Relief washed over Ihfaaz, making him feel lightheaded. The plan had worked. They had done it. He closed his eyes for a moment, letting out a breath he didn't know he was holding.

"Ihfaaz, you must come to our house for dinner tonight," she continued, her voice now filled with joy. "We want to thank you properly."

A smile spread across Ihfaaz's face. "Of course, Aunty. I'll be there."

As he ended the call, Dinu Kaka looked at him expectantly. "Good news?" he asked, sensing the change in Ihfaaz's attitude.

"Yes, very good news," Ihfaaz replied, feeling the weight that had been pressing on his chest finally lift. "Inspector Patil's son has been cleared. He's going back to college."

Dinu Kaka nodded, a slow smile spreading across his face. "Well done, Ihfaaz. You've done a great thing."

Ihfaaz nodded, a sense of satisfaction washing over him. For the first time in a while, it felt like things were going right. As he prepared to head to Inspector Patil's house for dinner, a smile played on his lips. His thoughts drifted to his encounter with Rajendra Desai a week ago, the moment he knew the plan had turned in their favour.

Chapter 19

On the fifth morning after his meeting with Pradip, Ihfaaz received a call. After a brief exchange, Ihfaaz knew he needed to head to Pune immediately. They arranged a lunch meeting at a discreet restaurant where Pradip filled him in on Rajendra Desai.

Rajendra had a modest background and wasn't particularly bright in his studies. His biggest accomplishment in college was falling in love with Radhika, the only daughter of Suryakant Joshi, a multimillionaire with a diverse business portfolio. Suryakant was also a trustee at the college where Inspector Patil's son was studying. Rajendra married Radhika and soon became involved in his father-in-law's business, eventually taking over the operations. Over time, Rajendra also took Suryakant's place on the college management committee.

As Pradip finished, he reached into his pocket and pulled out a small, nondescript pen drive, sliding it across the table to Ihfaaz. "This," Pradip said quietly, "has some photographs that might interest you. They're of Rajendra, in some... compromising situations. They were taken in some rather exclusive private parties. If these ever got out, it could spell the end of Rajendra's reputation and his hold on the college."

Ihfaaz picked up the pen drive, his mind churning with possibilities. The images on this drive could provide the leverage he needed to ensure a favourable decision from the college disciplinary committee. With this in hand, Ihfaaz knew he was ready to take the next step. It was time to make his move, and he planned to do it that very night.

Rajendra Desai had a late-night dinner meeting at one of the city's upscale restaurants. As he exited, he was in a jovial mood, the effects of good food, expensive wine, and pleasant company still lingering.

Approaching his favourite BMW SUV, he noticed someone casually leaning against the hood, smoking a cigarette. Rajendra felt a flicker of irritation. Nobody had the right to loiter around his car, especially not with a cigarette. As he neared, the smoker flicked the cigarette away and straightened up, moving away from the car.

Rajendra smirked, pleased to see his presence commanding respect. He relished the power he held over others. He unlocked the car with a press of his key fob, the vehicle's lights flashing in response. As he reached to open the driver's side door, his hand froze in mid-air. A figure stepped in front of him, blocking his way.

Before Rajendra could react, the man spoke. "Hey, Mr. Desai," the stranger said with a smirk. "Does your wife know about your side activities with her friend, Mrs. Sethi?"

Rajendra's eyes widened in surprise. He was used to dealing with many people, but this was different. The mention of Mrs. Sethi hit him like a slap. Regaining his composure, he glared at the man and unleashed a string of abuses. But the stranger didn't flinch. He simply stood there, smiling, as if he knew something Rajendra didn't.

"Calm down, Mr. Desai," the man said, his voice smooth and unbothered. "I'm not here to blackmail you. I just need a small favour. A clean chit for a student in the upcoming disciplinary committee meeting."

Rajendra's face contorted with rage. "You think you can blackmail me into helping some lowlife?" he spat. "I'll make sure that student's academic career is over, thanks to you."

The man's expression didn't change. He seemed unfazed by the threats. "You could do that," he said calmly, "but that would only work if you still had your seat on the management committee. Especially once the other members learn about your little boyfriend."

The colour drained from Rajendra's face. His anger was replaced with a look of sheer panic. This was a secret he had kept buried deep, one that no one knew except him and his boyfriend. The alcohol in his system seemed to evaporate instantly, replaced by cold, hard fear.

The stranger, still calm and collected, took out his phone. “Here,” he said, showing Rajendra a series of photographs. They were clear, incriminating, leaving no room for doubt. Rajendra’s eyes darted from the phone to the man’s face, shock and disbelief written all over him.

The man’s tone shifted, now cold and authoritative. “Your secret will stay safe with me,” he said. “I had no intention of revealing it, but your reaction leaves me no choice. All you need to do is give a clean chit to the student whose name is on this paper.”

He handed Rajendra a piece of paper. “Once the boy is cleared, this conversation never happened. And you’ll have earned yourself a favour from me. I know how to return favours, Mr. Desai.”

Rajendra’s mind raced, but he knew he had no choice. The photographs were too damning, the risk too great. He nodded, his voice barely a whisper. “Alright,” he said, taking the paper. “I’ll do it.”

With a final nod, the man turned and walked away, leaving Rajendra standing by his car, the weight of the encounter pressing heavily on him. He had no choice but to comply, and as he watched Ihfaaz disappear into the night, he knew that his life would never quite be the same.

The phone call from Mrs. Patil confirmed that Rajendra Desai had indeed kept his word. A sense of relief washed over Ihfaaz as he made his way to the Patil household, where he was greeted warmly. There was a slight awkwardness in Giriraj Patil’s manner, the history between them casting a subtle shadow over the evening. But for now, the tensions were set aside. Ihfaaz congratulated Giriraj Patil, who offered a curt nod in response, and then he turned his attention to Inspector Patil’s son, discussing his plans for the future.

After a lavish dinner, as the rest of the family retired to the living room, Ihfaaz and Giriraj Patil moved to the gallery. The cool night air was refreshing, and the faint sound of crickets chirping filled the silence as they smoked together, a shared vice that somehow broke the lingering tension.

"I have to thank you for what you did," Giriraj Patil said, his voice low. "You saved my son's future. I won't forget this."

Ihfaaz shook his head. "No need to consider this as a favour, sir," he replied. Reaching into his jacket, he pulled out an envelope and handed it to Giriraj Patil.

"What's this?" Giriraj asked, taking the envelope with a frown. He opened it to find it stuffed with cash—five lakh rupees.

"I can't accept this," Giriraj said, immediately handing it back. "You've already done more than enough."

But Ihfaaz insisted, pushing the envelope back into his hands. "Please, keep it. I know there are others in the department who need their share from the case. This is to make sure everything is handled smoothly. Consider it a part of the deal."

Giriraj Patil hesitated for a moment, then nodded, understanding the unspoken implications. "Alright," he agreed, pocketing the envelope. "I'll make sure it's distributed as needed."

They both took a long drag from their cigarettes, the smoke swirling in the cool night air. For a moment, they sat in silence, both lost in their thoughts.

"You don't have to worry about anything from the police front, at least for the time being," Giriraj Patil assured him finally, breaking the silence. "I'll keep things in check."

"Thank you, Sir," Ihfaaz said, genuinely grateful. He had earned a powerful ally, one who could make a significant difference in the days to come.

The tension between them had dissipated, replaced by a mutual understanding and a fledgling bond forged out of necessity. As they sat in the dim light of the gallery, two men from different worlds found common ground, each knowing that this was just the beginning of a new, complicated relationship.

Chapter 20

The next morning, Ihfaaz and Dinu Kaka sat together in their usual spot, savouring their hot cups of tea. The early morning sun cast a gentle glow over the city, making the moment feel calm and serene.

Dinu Kaka broke the silence, his voice filled with curiosity. "How did dinner go last night?"

Ihfaaz took a sip of his tea, considering his words before responding. "It went well. I congratulated Inspector Patil and talked with his son about his future plans. After dinner, Inspector Patil and I had a private conversation. I thanked him for his help and gave him five lakhs."

Dinu Kaka's eyebrows shot up in surprise. "Five lakhs? Why did you give him so much?"

Ihfaaz nodded, understanding Dinu Kaka's concern. "It was necessary, Dinu Kaka. The money wasn't just for Inspector Patil. It's for the others in his department too. If Patil kept all the money for himself, the others would think he was being greedy and would be less cooperative. We needed to spread it around to keep everyone quiet and to make sure the case against me doesn't come back to bite us."

Dinu Kaka leaned back in his chair, a thoughtful look on his face. He sighed, then nodded slowly. "You did the right thing, Ihfaaz. In our line of work, keeping everyone happy is crucial. If the others in the department feel they've been left out, it could cause more problems for us. Five lakhs is a small price to pay for keeping things smooth."

Ihfaaz felt a sense of relief at Dinu Kaka's approval. But there was still something important he needed to share. "Dinu Kaka, there's something else I need to tell you."

"What is it?" Dinu Kaka asked, his eyes narrowing slightly.

"I found out who tipped off the police about you," Ihfaaz said, his voice low. "It was our landlord. He wants us out of the office. He thought bringing the police down on us would force you to leave."

Dinu Kaka's face darkened, his expression hardening. But then he sighed, a weary look in his eyes. "I always had a feeling that man was up to no good. The landlord has wanted this place for a long time. But with the police backing off now, we've bought ourselves some time."

Ihfaaz nodded, sensing that Dinu Kaka was more troubled than he let on. The recent events had clearly taken a toll on him, and Ihfaaz couldn't help but feel concern for the older man. They sat in silence for a moment, the weight of their conversation lingering in the air, as Ihfaaz wondered what Dinu Kaka might decide to do next.

Dinu Kaka absently fiddled with his cup, lost in thought, before finally addressing Ihfaaz. "You know, my son isn't interested in the hawala business, and to be honest, I don't want him involved in it either. This line of work... it's not for everyone, especially not for him. He's shown interest in the courier business, and that's a good, honest living."

He paused, his voice trembling slightly as he continued. "This last episode with the police... it's shaken me, Ihfaaz. If it hadn't been for you, I'd have been in serious trouble. I'm not as young as I used to be, and the stress is getting to me. I've decided to close down the hawala operations and focus on the courier business. It's safer, and with you and my son on board, we can really grow it. But... I wanted to ask your opinion."

Ihfaaz remained silent for a moment, his face thoughtful. He took a deep breath before responding, "Dinu Kaka, if you're sure about stepping away, what if I took over the hawala operation? You could focus on the courier business with your son, and I could manage the hawala side. I've learned a lot from you, and I'm ready to handle the risks. I'll make sure you still get a share of the income, like a royalty for all the guidance you've given me."

Dinu Kaka was taken aback. He hadn't expected Ihfaaz to offer to take over the risky part of the business. "Ihfaaz, you're young. This business is full of stress and danger. You've seen what happened recently—do you really want to deal with that on your own?"

"I understand the risks, Dinu Kaka," Ihfaaz replied firmly. "But I also see the opportunity. I have my reasons for needing to stay involved in this kind of work. And with you focusing on the courier business, it'll give both of us a chance to do what we're best at. I can handle the hawala side, and you can scale up the courier business. Together, we can make sure both sides thrive."

Dinu Kaka saw the determination in Ihfaaz's eyes. Despite his concerns, he knew that Ihfaaz was capable and had proven his loyalty time and again. Finally, he nodded. "Alright, Ihfaaz. If this is what you want, then we'll do it. We'll run the operations separately from now on. I'll focus on the courier business, and you take over the hawala. But promise me, you'll be careful."

Ihfaaz smiled, relieved. "I promise, Dinu Kaka. I'll be careful, and I'll make sure everything runs smoothly. We'll make this work, together."

They clinked their tea cups together, sealing the deal, each aware that they were stepping into a new chapter—one that held its own set of challenges and opportunities.

Chapter 21

Given the illegal nature of hawala, keeping the identities of both senders and receivers secret is crucial. When Ihfaaz was caught, all of Dinu Kaka's clients were worried. They feared that Ihfaaz might reveal their names or, worse, that the police would gain access to their transaction records. However, Ihfaaz remained tight-lipped. Despite enduring intense torture, he did not divulge any client names. As for the transaction records, the cyber department's efforts to decrypt the files were in vain. They couldn't extract any data from the highly encrypted files Ihfaaz had set up.

This steadfastness and loyalty earned Ihfaaz a lot of respect. Word spread quickly in business circles that Ihfaaz was a stand-up guy who wouldn't break under pressure. His reputation grew—he was known as someone who could be trusted, even in the direst situations.

When clients heard that Ihfaaz had started the hawala business on his own, they felt reassured. They knew they could trust him to keep their identities safe. Not only did the regular clients return, but Ihfaaz also attracted many new clients who were eager to do business with someone so reliable. His reputation for discretion and his ability to handle pressure made him a sought-after figure in the business network.

Business was booming, and Ihfaaz's name became synonymous with trustworthiness and resilience in these circles. His decision to take over the hawala operation had paid off, and he was quickly establishing himself as a powerful player in the business.

Within a span of a few months, the hawala business under Ihfaaz progressed to new heights. Existing clients recommended him to new clients, and the influx of business required additional manpower.

Ihfaaz offered Pradip Wakode the position of manager, even if it meant relocating to Mumbai. Having already worked with Ihfaaz, Pradip readily agreed to shift base to Mumbai.

Another advantage of the booming business was the diverse range of people Ihfaaz got to interact with. He had firsthand access to the latest happenings in the business world. With his contact in the police department through Inspector Patil, Ihfaaz was able to help settle minor disputes between businessmen, further cementing his reputation as a trustworthy and resourceful individual in business circles.

The biggest problem with earning money isn't just making it—it's saving and investing it safely. This risk multiplies when the money is earned illegally. With his regular interactions in the business and police circles, Ihfaaz quickly realized this fact. His sharp mind spotted a business opportunity in helping others invest and launder their black money safely. This new venture could potentially provide a secure avenue for his clients to grow their wealth while keeping it hidden from prying eyes. Ihfaaz knew that if he played his cards right, he could establish himself as a key figure in this shadowy world, ensuring not only his success but also the trust and loyalty of his clients.

The first opportunity for Ihfaaz's new venture came from a regular customer, a seasoned bullion trader. During one of their usual conversations, the trader casually mentioned his belief that silver prices were set to skyrocket in the coming months. Ihfaaz, sensing a potential opportunity, asked if the trader would be willing to hold silver on his behalf if he decided to invest. The trader, eager to earn favour with Ihfaaz bhai, readily agreed.

After the trader left, Ihfaaz made a quick call to Inspector Patil. He explained the silver opportunity, emphasizing the potential for quick profits. Patil thought it over for a moment and then agreed to invest ₹2.5 lakhs. Ihfaaz immediately placed an order with the bullion trader to buy silver at the current market price.

A short while later, Inspector Patil called back, asking if the deal could be extended to a couple of his friends. Ihfaaz agreed but stipulated a 15% commission on any profits earned. After some negotiation, they finalized an additional investment of ₹10 lakhs. Ihfaaz promptly bought silver for the full amount, confident in the trader's reliability; he knew the trader handled large sums for him regularly.

Now, it was a matter of waiting. Ihfaaz crossed his fingers as he watched the market. The prices initially rose slowly but then picked up momentum. Within a month, the value of the silver surged, resulting in a handsome return of around 18%. Satisfied, Ihfaaz sold the entire stock, returning the capital plus profit to Inspector Patil and the other investors, minus his 15% commission.

Inspector Patil and his friends were thrilled with their earnings and urged Ihfaaz to inform them of any similar opportunities in the future. This successful transaction gave Ihfaaz the confidence to explore this new avenue of investment, combining it with his established hawala business.

Chapter 22

Two years later

Ihfaaz's hawala and trading businesses were not just thriving; they were becoming cornerstones of a burgeoning underground economy. The hawala network had grown substantially, attracting the interest of various influential figures, including high-ranking police officers, bureaucrats, and other government officials. The discreet nature of Ihfaaz's operations, combined with his reputation for reliability and discretion, made his services highly sought after. What began as a modest operation was now a vast network of transactions, with money flowing in and out with remarkable efficiency.

The success of Ihfaaz's hawala operations soon opened doors to new ventures. Ihfaaz's keen eye for opportunity led him to expand his activities into trading, initially in precious metals like silver and gold, which were seen as safe havens for unaccounted cash. These investments quickly paid off, earning substantial returns that bolstered Ihfaaz's capital reserves. Over time, Ihfaaz diversified further, branching out into other commodities and avenues, each investment meticulously calculated to maximize profits.

As word spread about Ihfaaz's success, more and more business owners, from small entrepreneurs to large corporate players, sought his expertise. Many of these businesses were struggling with liquidity problems, particularly those operating in sectors prone to fluctuations, such as real estate, construction, and import-export. Ihfaaz's offer of cash injections was a lifeline, allowing these businesses to stay afloat. In return, Ihfaaz negotiated favourable terms that ensured substantial returns on his investments, securing both his profit margins and the loyalty of his clients.

Ihfaaz's also made strategic investments in legitimate businesses, blurring the lines between his illicit and legal enterprises. This dual approach provided him with an aura of respectability while safeguarding his interests on both fronts. His growing influence attracted smaller hawala operators, who, recognizing his dominance, sought partnerships. These alliances further extended Ihfaaz's reach, giving him access to a broader client base and facilitating a steady flow of cash that fuelled his investment operations.

With the rapid expansion of his businesses came the need for a more robust infrastructure. The small office space that had once sufficed was no longer adequate. Ihfaaz invested in a larger, more sophisticated office, equipped with the latest technology to handle the volume of transactions and ensure the security of sensitive information. He understood that the backbone of his operations was not just in the secrecy of the hawala transactions but also in maintaining the trust of his clients, which required airtight security and absolute confidentiality.

Recognizing the growing demands on his time and resources, Ihfaaz expanded his staff, carefully selecting individuals who were not only skilled but also trustworthy and discreet. Among the new hires was Nadia D'Souza, a sharp and efficient office assistant. Nadia quickly proved indispensable, managing the day-to-day operations with a level of precision that freed Ihfaaz to focus on strategic decisions and new opportunities. Her ability to handle sensitive information discreetly and her organizational skills made her a key player in Ihfaaz's expanding empire.

Nadia's role extended beyond administrative duties. She became Ihfaaz's confidante and right-hand person, assisting in handling client relations, organizing meetings, and ensuring that all transactions were executed smoothly. Her presence allowed Ihfaaz to project a professional and organized image, further enhancing his reputation in the business circles.

As Ihfaaz's empire grew, so did his network of contacts. He regularly interacted with influential figures, gathering valuable insights into the latest market trends and potential opportunities. His contacts in the police department proved particularly beneficial, offering him a direct line to the police department. This connection allowed Ihfaaz to mediate and settle disputes between businessmen discreetly, avoiding unnecessary confrontations and ensuring that all parties remained satisfied. It was a mutually beneficial relationship; Ihfaaz's influence kept the police off his back, while his financial acumen provided opportunities for profit that were too tempting to ignore.

The intertwining of legal and illegal enterprises, the strategic alliances with powerful figures, and the ever-expanding network of clients made Ihfaaz a formidable force in the shadowy world of underground finance. His ability to adapt, innovate, and seize opportunities ensured that his empire continued to grow, solidifying his position as a key player in both the legitimate and clandestine business communities. As his influence spread, Ihfaaz knew that the future held even more possibilities, and he was ready to capitalize on them, one calculated move at a time.

Chapter 23

These financial transactions brought with them invaluable contacts, weaving Ihfaaz into the fabric of powerful and influential networks. His clients, recognizing the value of his connections and problem-solving abilities, were always eager to gain his favour and, if possible, become closer to him. A close friend like Ihfaaz was an asset to anyone navigating the complexities of both legal and illegal ventures.

Whenever his clients faced a problem, be it a minor inconvenience or a significant hurdle, they would confide in Ihfaaz, trusting his ability to find a solution. Often, the answer lay within Ihfaaz's extensive network of contacts or through a connection known to those contacts. Ihfaaz's ability to navigate these connections effectively turned him into a problem-solver of sorts, a figure who could make things happen when others saw only roadblocks.

For those who brought their problems to Ihfaaz and found solutions, there was a sense of deep gratitude and loyalty. They carried with them a lifelong goodwill and benefaction towards Ihfaaz, knowing that he had the power to change their fortunes. On the other hand, those who provided solutions felt honoured to have been able to offer their services to Ihfaaz, gaining a sense of pride from being useful to a man of his stature. This mutual exchange of favours created a powerful bond of reciprocity and loyalty, further solidifying Ihfaaz's influence and reputation.

The nature of the work he facilitated varied widely. Sometimes it was something as simple as securing a bed in a crowded hospital, a seemingly impossible task in a city teeming with people. At other times, it was getting someone's child admitted to a prestigious college, cutting through the red tape and bureaucratic hurdles that would otherwise stand in the way. Whether the task was small or significant, Ihfaaz had the resources and connections to make it happen.

In every sense of the word, Ihfaaz became the *Facilitator*. His reputation grew as the man who could fix any problem, solve any issue, and make the impossible possible. He was the one people turned to when they needed something done—efficiently, quietly, and effectively. Through this role, Ihfaaz amassed not just wealth, but power, influence, and respect. His network expanded, his influence grew, and his name became synonymous with capability and resourcefulness. In a world full of complexities and uncertainties, Ihfaaz was the one constant—the facilitator who could always be counted on to deliver.

Dinu Kaka and his son, Samir, were also pleased with the way Ihfaaz was helping them expand their courier business. Thanks to Ihfaaz's vast network and influence, he secured a steady stream of business for Dinu Kaka, ensuring that their operations never ran dry. His connections proved invaluable, opening doors to new clients and business opportunities that Dinu Kaka could have only dreamed of before. The courier business flourished under this newfound momentum, and both father and son found themselves busier than ever.

Despite his growing empire and the increasing demands on his time, Ihfaaz always made it a point to meet with Dinu Kaka two to three times a week. These meetings weren't just about business; they were an opportunity for camaraderie, sharing news, and offering advice. Ihfaaz valued these sessions as a chance to connect with the man who had given him his start in Mumbai, showing genuine respect and gratitude for Dinu Kaka's guidance and support. Ihfaaz treated Dinu Kaka like a mentor and Samir like a younger brother, fostering a sense of family among them.

Dinu Kaka was touched by the respect Ihfaaz showed him, knowing that it wasn't just out of obligation but genuine regard. He appreciated how Ihfaaz always sought his opinion and involved him in important decisions, valuing his experience and wisdom. It warmed his heart to see how Ihfaaz took Samir under his wing, guiding him through the complexities of the business world. Samir, in turn, looked up to Ihfaaz, learning from him and striving to emulate his success and behaviour.

During their meetings, Dinu Kaka often shared snippets of advice with Ihfaaz, drawing from his years of experience in business and life. These nuggets of wisdom, whether about handling tricky clients, managing staff, or navigating the undercurrents of business circles, were always appreciated by Ihfaaz. He knew that Dinu Kaka's insights were invaluable, offering perspectives that only years of experience could provide.

The bond between them grew stronger with each passing day, built on mutual respect, trust, and a shared vision for success. Ihfaaz's success was their success, and together, they navigated the challenges and opportunities that came their way. For Dinu Kaka, seeing Ihfaaz rise to prominence while still holding onto his roots and values was a source of immense pride. It reminded him that even in a world driven by power and money, respect and loyalty still held great value.

Getting entry into Ihfaaz's network of investors was not easy. Prospective members had to be vouched for by at least one existing member, ensuring that the syndicate remained secure and exclusive. This referral system created a chain of trust, preventing any untoward individuals from joining the network. Additionally, only Ihfaaz or his close confidantes knew the identities of all the investors, providing a layer of security that made members feel safe, knowing their involvement was kept confidential.

Ihfaaz was constantly on the lookout for ways to refine and improve his business practices. He was keenly aware of the risks involved in his line of work, especially when dealing with large sums of unaccounted cash and investments. His sharp mind was always at work, finding means to make his operations not just safer but also sleeker and, wherever possible, more aligned with legal frameworks.

To navigate the complex landscape of laws and regulations, Ihfaaz assembled a team of top-notch lawyers and chartered accountants. These professionals were not just advisors; they were crucial allies in his quest to maintain and expand his empire. They provided insights into tax laws, loopholes, investment strategies, and ways to mitigate legal risks. Ihfaaz understood the value of their expertise and made it a point to stay deeply involved in their work.

Every week or fortnight, depending on his schedule, Ihfaaz would sit down with each member of his legal and financial team individually. These meetings were more than just routine check-ins; they were brainstorming sessions where ideas flowed freely. Ihfaaz would probe them for insights, challenge their assumptions, and seek their advice on various aspects of his operations. This collaborative approach allowed him to gain a deeper understanding of the intricacies of law and finance, ensuring that he was always a step ahead.

These sessions were instrumental in shaping the way Ihfaaz conducted his business. They helped him refine his strategies, identify potential risks, and explore new avenues for growth. Over time, Ihfaaz's operations became a model of efficiency and discretion, with a keen focus on legality wherever possible. His syndicate was not just about making money; it was about creating a sustainable and resilient network that could withstand scrutiny and adapt to changing circumstances.

By constantly refining his business model and staying informed about the latest legal and financial developments, Ihfaaz ensured that his empire remained robust and resilient. His commitment to continuous improvement made him a formidable player in the business circles, respected not just for his wealth but for his intelligence and foresight.

During his brainstorming sessions with his team of legal and financial advisors, Ihfaaz had a breakthrough idea—creating shell companies to manage and launder the money his syndicate was generating. He started forming private limited companies with like-minded investors who were comfortable with each other. These companies were structured to have a nominal sum of capital, pooled in by the investors. Interestingly, it wasn't necessary for the actual investors to be the listed shareholders; the choice of shareholder names was left to the investors themselves.

In each of these shell companies, Ihfaaz maintained a minimum 5% stake and held a general power of attorney, granting him the authority to act on behalf of all shareholders. The real genius of this strategy came when a legitimate company needed liquid cash. That's when one of the shell companies would step in, purchasing a mutually agreed-upon percentage of shares at face value through official banking channels. The difference between the face value and the actual agreed price was paid in cash, split among the shareholders of the shell company.

This approach allowed the target company to receive a much-needed cash infusion, while the investors in the shell company secured their investments through legitimate shareholdings. Over time, if any investor wished to exit, they could sell their stake at market value, partially in cash and partially by cheque. This process gradually legitimized the laundered money as the legal valuation aspect overshadowed the initial cash component.

By holding 5% to 20% in all these companies, without needing to invest his own money, Ihfaaz significantly boosted his wealth. His role in laundering the money, coordinating between investors, and finding profitable deals was invaluable, leading to substantial profits for everyone involved. This strategy was a win-win for all parties, further solidifying Ihfaaz's reputation as a masterful facilitator in his network.

Everything seemed to be falling into place for Ihfaaz. The money was flowing in from all corners of the country, his operations were expanding, and his reputation was solid. Yet, despite the smooth sailing, Ihfaaz felt a nagging sense that something was missing. He couldn't quite put his finger on it, but he knew there was a critical piece of the puzzle that had yet to fall into place.

Chapter 24

It took a couple of years for the opportunity to reveal itself, and it happened where he least expected it. Ihfaaz travelled to Sultanabad to attend the wedding of his partner's daughter. Sultanabad was a city that intrigued him—it wasn't too big, yet not too small, bearing a quiet, unassuming charm that reminded him of his hometown, Kushalgram.

During the wedding festivities, his host, the father of the bride and his business partner, requested that Ihfaaz stay for an extra day, hinting at something important he wanted to discuss. Though curious, Ihfaaz maintained his gracious demeanour and agreed to extend his stay. He knew better than to rush; sometimes, the best opportunities came when least expected. Little did he know, this conversation would lead him to the missing piece of the puzzle he had been seeking.

The next day, Ihfaaz woke up late, feeling relaxed after the previous night's festivities. After a leisurely breakfast, he began attending to various phone calls, managing the stream of business that never quite slowed down, even when he was away from his usual base. As he was wrapping up a call, his partner, Niranjan Shriwas, arrived to meet him.

Ihfaaz greeted Niranjan with warmth and respect, addressing him as "Niranjan ji," a mark of the deep regard he had for the older man. After the usual pleasantries and small talk, Niranjan gently steered the conversation to the main reason he had asked Ihfaaz to stay an extra day.

"There's something serious I need to discuss with you, Ihfaaz Bhai," Niranjan began, his tone more sombre than before. He explained that there was a local co-operative credit society based in Sultanabad, the Mahasampada Co-operative Credit Society, which was in deep trouble.

The society had been poorly managed for years, and now it was on the brink of collapse. Financial mismanagement, coupled with some shady dealings, had left the society in a precarious position.

Niranjan continued, "The managing director of the society, along with the other board members, has reached out to me, desperate for help. If the law enforcement agencies get involved, it will be a disaster. They're terrified that not only will they be arrested and disgraced, but there's a real chance they could face imprisonment."

He paused, letting the gravity of the situation sink in. "They've asked me if I could find a way to pull them out of this mess, to prevent this from becoming a public scandal. And I think you might be the only person who can really help them, given your expertise and your... connections."

Niranjan looked at Ihfaaz intently, waiting for his response, knowing that the younger man had a knack for turning crises into opportunities.

After returning to Mumbai the next morning, Ihfaaz wasted no time. He immediately called an urgent meeting with Nadia and Pradip. As they gathered, Ihfaaz, with a gleam in his eye, broke the news: they were going to invest in and take over a co-operative credit society in Sultanabad.

Nadia, accustomed to unusual investments, felt the urge to let Ihfaaz explain. Pradip, on the other hand, was taken aback and immediately started firing questions. "A co-operative credit society? You went to Sultanabad for a wedding, and now this?" His mind raced, trying to connect the dots.

Ihfaaz, maintaining his calm, told Pradip to slow down and then shared the entire story of Mahasampada Co-operative Credit Society. He explained how the society was on the brink of collapse, desperate for cash, and riddled with financial mismanagement. "But why us?" Pradip asked, still unconvinced.

"They're short on cash, about to go under," Ihfaaz replied. "And we can turn this into an opportunity."

"How big is the hole?" Pradip asked, his voice laced with concern.

Ihfaaz smiled. "It's not a hole, it's a crater. Rs. 35 crores."

Both Nadia and Pradip were stunned. The sheer scale of the investment was staggering. Why take such a risk? Ihfaaz, as always, had already thought it through. He explained that this was the first step in legitimizing their business operations. By taking control of the credit society, they could secure a legitimate financial front for their transactions.

"The first thing we'll do," Ihfaaz elaborated, "is ask our current clients to invest in the society—current and fixed deposits. That will stabilize the society for now." He then looked at Pradip. "You'll travel to Sultanabad and take over operations there. The current board is fully cooperative, and they've agreed to step down whenever we ask."

He laid out the detailed plan, explaining how they would use the co-operative society as a front to launder money, bring in fresh capital, and safeguard their illicit earnings under a legitimate umbrella. Slowly, Pradip and Nadia began to grasp the brilliance behind the move. What initially seemed like an unnecessary risk now looked like a masterstroke.

After the meeting, Ihfaaz held another long session with his lawyers and chartered accountants, refining the legal details. Pradip and Nadia came in and out of the conference room as required, each gaining a clearer picture of their respective roles in the plan. A couple of days later, Pradip left for Sultanabad to take over the society's operations.

What none of them knew at the time was that this move would eventually lead to the entire operation shifting to Sultanabad, setting the stage for a new chapter in Ihfaaz's expanding empire.

A month after Pradip had taken over the management of the Mahasampada Co-operative Credit Society, Ihfaaz made another visit to Sultanabad to assess the progress. On paper, the society's finances had improved considerably compared to the dire situation they were in before. The board of directors, once anxious about their potential downfall, were now relaxed and content, believing that the worst was behind them. The staff, too, had a renewed sense of stability, as word spread that the crisis had been averted.

As Ihfaaz toured the branch alongside the chairman, manager, and Pradip, he listened intently, absorbing every detail about the society's operations. His face remained noncommittal, giving away nothing, but his sharp mind was meticulously processing the information. After the tour, they all headed to lunch, where the atmosphere was casual yet charged with anticipation. Everyone was eager to know what Ihfaaz thought of their progress.

After lunch, however, the tone shifted. Ihfaaz informed the managing director that the time had come for the current board to step down and hand over full control of the society to him and his team. Though the board had agreed to this arrangement earlier, the managing director now hesitated, feeling the weight of the decision. But one look at Ihfaaz's resolute expression convinced him that arguing further would be futile. Reluctantly, he agreed, and the transition of power was complete.

Once the formalities were out of the way, Ihfaaz and Pradip retreated to the privacy of the hotel room. This was where the real planning would unfold. Sitting across from Pradip, Ihfaaz began laying out the changes he wanted to implement to cement their control over the co-operative society.

First, the entire IT infrastructure of the society would be upgraded. The outdated software currently in use would be replaced with a more sophisticated system sourced from someone within the syndicate. This new software would be programmed with hidden functionalities, allowing for any data to be added, deleted, or modified without the knowledge of the staff. Furthermore, physical access to the server would be strictly controlled by Ihfaaz's team, and the server itself would be relocated to a separate site for maximum control and security.

Next, Ihfaaz proposed a bold financial strategy: the society would offer higher deposit rates to attract more clients and lower interest rates to remain competitive. This would draw a larger influx of clients, eager to take advantage of favourable terms. This move would not only bring in more deposits but also provide the capital needed to expand their operations swiftly.

Expansion was key. Ihfaaz directed Pradip to start aggressively expanding the branch network, extending the society's reach beyond Sultanabad to other strategic locations. This would not only enhance their legitimacy but also broaden the avenues for their operations.

Finally, and most critically, Ihfaaz emphasized the need for Pradip to keep an eye out for similar opportunities. The acquisition of other struggling co-operative societies should be prioritized, but the ultimate goal would be to acquire a full-fledged bank. That would be the crown jewel, giving them a legal platform to operate on a much larger scale and with greater freedom. The transformation of the society into a legitimate front for their operations would be complete.

Pradip, listening to the plan, understood the brilliance of it. Each step was carefully calculated to expand their empire, legitimize their operations, and increase their influence in the financial world. As he left the hotel room, he knew that this was only the beginning of a much larger game that Ihfaaz was playing.

What neither of them realized at that moment was how far-reaching the consequences of these decisions would be, and how they would change the face of their business in ways they hadn't fully anticipated.

Chapter 25

Five years had passed since Ahsan, now known as Ihfaaz, left behind his former life in Kushalgram and disappeared from the world, faking his own death to escape a web of betrayal. During these years, Mumbai had become his new home, a city where his ambition took root and flourished. He kept in regular contact with his mother, but even she remained in the dark about his whereabouts and the empire he was building. The scars of his past, coupled with his burning desire for revenge, kept him focused on his mission—one that he vowed would culminate in his return to prove his innocence and settle scores with those who had wronged him.

Family updates were bittersweet. His father, though still engaged in business, had largely handed over control to Ahsan's brothers. His younger sister was now married and happy. The family had grown, and Ahsan had become an uncle as his siblings welcomed children. His mother frequently pleaded with him to consider marriage, to settle down in some way, even if not back in Kushalgram. She often reminded him of the joys of family and the importance of love, but those pleas fell on deaf ears. The part of Ahsan that was capable of love and warmth had withered away long ago. The flame that once might have sought happiness in family life had been consumed by the fire of ambition and vengeance.

For Ahsan—now Ihfaaz—there was no room for softness, no space for emotions that could weaken his resolve. All that was left within him was a fierce hunger for power and a deep, simmering rage that drove him forward.

Ihfaaz's long wait to take over a full-fledged bank finally came to an end after two and a half years. The story of **Unity Co-operative Bank**, based in Nagpur, was eerily similar to the one he had faced with the co-operative society in Sultanabad. Like the society, the bank had fallen into a severe cash crunch, its financial woes leaving the management desperate for a saviour. Sensing another opportunity, Ihfaaz swooped in, offering a bailout—but it came with a tough and hard bargain. The terms were in his favour, and the bank had little choice but to accept.

Once again, Ihfaaz entrusted Pradip Wakode with the responsibility of taking over the bank's operations. Under Pradip's oversight, fresh funds were injected, and the team mobilized deposits. Within a matter of days, the financial crises that had plagued Unity Co-operative Bank seemed to disappear. A fortnight later, the bank's problems were a thing of the past, and within the next month, the existing board of directors resigned, clearing the way for Ihfaaz to install his own trusted team.

This takeover was more than just another acquisition for Ihfaaz—it was a strategic leap. With control over a co-operative bank, his influence in the financial sector deepened. The bank, though small, opened new doors to expand his operations, moving him closer to his ultimate goal of legitimizing his empire while keeping his network and operations intact behind the scenes.

Nagpur, like Sultanabad, became another stronghold in Ihfaaz's ever-expanding web.

The entire template Ihfaaz had successfully implemented at the co-operative credit society in Sultanabad was seamlessly replicated at **Unity Co-operative Bank**. The IT infrastructure was the first to receive an overhaul, and, once again, the software was sourced from a trusted firm within the syndicate. This software was no ordinary system—it was designed with precision and purpose. It allowed remote manipulation of the bank's database, ensuring that any adjustments or changes could be made at will without the knowledge of the bank's staff. To ensure maximum security, the server was relocated to a secure, undisclosed location, with access restricted to only a select few from Ihfaaz's inner circle. These individuals had no official connection to either the bank or the co-operative society, ensuring plausible deniability.

The bank, along with the co-operative credit society, became a perfect front for storing and processing unaccounted cash. Through the specially designed software, a myriad of fake accounts were created in the system—each of which was used to "adjust" the additional cash that flowed in through the hawala network. This method enabled Ihfaaz to keep the cash circulating in and out of the financial system without raising suspicions.

To further streamline the operation, special ATM cards were issued to regular customers involved in the hawala transactions. These customers would deposit unaccounted cash into one of the designated fake accounts. On the other end, the recipient of the hawala amount could simply visit the nearest ATM, withdraw the cash, and go on their way—no questions asked, no paper trail. It was a near-perfect system, one that allowed Ihfaaz to gain an edge over other hawala operators.

While this method elevated Ihfaaz's standing in the underground world of hawala, it also created a ripple of discontent among his competitors. His sophisticated system cut into the profits of several smaller hawala operators, who were now losing business to Ihfaaz's highly efficient and secure model. Some quietly backed off, unable to compete with the scale and technological advancement Ihfaaz had introduced, but others were not as forgiving. Disgruntled and threatened by his rise, these operators began watching Ihfaaz closely, their dissatisfaction brewing into resentment, planting the seeds for potential conflict in the future.

Despite the growing unease among his competitors, Ihfaaz remained an open-minded and cooperative figure in the hawala world. He had built a reputation not just for his efficiency but also for being someone willing to help fellow operators. However, as his influence expanded, not everyone appreciated his rise. About six months after launching the ATM service, an incident occurred that would further solidify his reputation as someone you didn't cross lightly.

Late one night, as Ihfaaz was leaving his office, a small-time thug cornered him in the dimly lit alleyway. With a knife pressed to his chest and a hard punch to his stomach, the thug issued a warning—demanding that Ihfaaz shut down his hawala operations or face severe consequences. Instead of showing fear, Ihfaaz found the situation almost amusing. He could have easily overpowered the thug, but instead, in a calm, soft tone, he asked, "What do you really want?"

The thug, thinking Ihfaaz was trying to act brave, repeated his demand. But Ihfaaz, unflinching, asked him how much cash he needed instead, making it clear that shutting down the business was not an option. The thug misread the situation, assuming Ihfaaz was bluffing. Pressing the knife a little harder into Ihfaaz's skin, he nicked the outer layer, but before he could fully realize the gravity of his mistake, everything changed.

Ihfaaz's calm appearance vanished in an instant, replaced by blazing anger. Within a heartbeat, he grabbed the thug's wrist, twisted it with precision, forcing a painful shriek that was stifled as Ihfaaz expertly squeezed his windpipe. The thug, gasping for air, soon lost consciousness, completely unaware of how quickly things had spiralled out of his control.

Calmly, Ihfaaz dialled a police officer he had on speed dial. Within minutes, a police van arrived, and the unconscious thug was taken away without a trace of the altercation left behind. The next day, the thug's family showed up at the police station, hoping to plead for leniency. To their shock, they discovered that in the span of 12 hours, their lives had been turned upside down. Their home had been repossessed, his elder brother was fired from his job at a local café, and they were warned that things would only get worse unless the thug revealed who had sent him.

Even the hardest criminals often break when their families are dragged into their mess. Realizing his mistake, the thug quickly confessed that he had been hired by one of Ihfaaz's competitors—a rival hawala operator who, unlike Ihfaaz, didn't understand the true extent of the danger he had invited by crossing him.

On Ihfaaz's instruction, no official charges were filed against the thug, and he was released. However, he was warned that if he ever came near Ihfaaz again, he wouldn't be walking out of a police station but heading straight to the morgue. As a parting gesture, the "unfortunate circumstances" surrounding the thug's family were lifted, their home returned, and his brother reinstated at the café within hours.

The rival hawala operator, however, wasn't as lucky. The very next day, multiple agencies raided his office, disrupting his operations. A fortnight later, the rival met with an "unfortunate" road accident that left him bedridden for the next 15 months. Though no one spoke openly of what had transpired, the message was clear to everyone in the underground circles: **you do not mess with Ihfaaz.**

Ihfaaz was kind and cooperative to those who treated him with respect, but cross him—and the consequences were brutal and long-lasting.

Chapter 26

As time passed, Ihfaaz began to feel that remaining in Mumbai brought more attention to his activities than was necessary. The city had served its purpose as a base for his rise, but now it felt too exposed, too scrutinized. He needed a quieter place to operate from, somewhere that reminded him of his roots without the constant pressure of prying eyes. Sultanabad seemed like the perfect choice. The town's familiar charm and slower pace evoked memories of Kushalgram, and it felt like a place where he could build further without the spotlight bearing down on him.

With his banking and hawala businesses running smoothly, Ihfaaz made the decision to relocate to Sultanabad. He instructed Pradip to divide his time between Mumbai and Sultanabad, managing the operations in both cities, while Ihfaaz would settle into his new base and only visit Mumbai when absolutely necessary.

What surprised Ihfaaz, however, was Nadia's insistence on joining him in Sultanabad. She had become indispensable to him over the years, not just as a competent administrator but as someone he had grown used to having by his side. Despite his usual reluctance to allow anyone too close, he agreed to her request. Nadia had proven her loyalty time and again, and her presence brought a sense of calm and efficiency to his operations. Together, they would begin the next chapter in Sultanabad.

Only Dinu Kaka was saddened by Ihfaaz's departure. With glistening eyes, he expressed how much he would miss Ihfaaz. Over the past seven years, the relationship between them had evolved into something deeper than just business. Dinu Kaka had developed a fatherly affection for Ihfaaz, and although he had once been curious about Ihfaaz's mysterious past, he had long since stopped asking. Their bond had transcended questions and suspicions.

For his part, Ihfaaz had done everything for Dinu Kaka that a devoted son might do for his father. From taking the blame during the police raid to scaling up the courier business for Samir, Ihfaaz had always put Dinu Kaka's interests first. Samir, under Ihfaaz's guidance and influence, had transformed his small courier company into a massive enterprise with a significant turnover and a widespread network of branches. When the e-commerce boom hit, Ihfaaz leveraged his connections to secure lucrative contracts for Samir's company, turning it into a logistics partner for all the major e-commerce platforms in the country. This catapulted the company's growth, and now Samir was even contemplating taking the company public.

Before leaving, Ihfaaz assured Dinu Kaka that he would visit often and never let Samir be exposed to harm. He made it clear that despite the physical distance, his protection and influence would continue to safeguard both Dinu Kaka and Samir.

As Ihfaaz prepared to leave for Sultanabad, the sense of a new chapter began to take shape. The move wasn't just about relocating his base of operations—it was a strategic shift, a step toward a more controlled and calculated future. In Sultanabad, he would build something larger, something more permanent, all while keeping a low profile. But as always with Ihfaaz, there were layers to every move he made. He knew that staying out of the spotlight didn't mean retreating—it meant waiting for the right moment to strike. And in Sultanabad, he could plan his next move, hidden from view yet always one step ahead.

Nadia's Story

Nadia sat by the window of her small room in the working women's hostel, her thoughts a tangled mess as the sounds of the city buzzed faintly outside. The grief from her father's death had dulled, but a new kind of ache had settled in its place. It was the pain of unrequited love—love she had offered to Ihfaaz, only to be met with calm rejection.

From a young age, Nadia's beauty had been a defining feature of her life. At every family function, festival, or gathering, relatives and strangers alike couldn't help but admire her. Her dusky skin had an inviting, earthy glow that set her apart, while her soft, delicate features gave her face a serene and calming presence. Her eyes, expressive yet gentle, seemed to reveal a depth of kindness and quiet strength, drawing people in without her saying a word. Framed by subtly arched brows, those eyes added a depth that few could resist.

Her cheeks had a natural, soft contour, giving her face graceful lines that complemented her full, understatedly charming lips. Every time she smiled—though rare these days—it was as if her entire face lit up, leaving a lasting impression of warmth and elegance. But the very beauty that everyone admired had become an obstacle in her life, especially after her mother passed away and her father succumbed to alcoholism.

After her mother's death, when her father became too lost in the bottle to care for either of them, Nadia had tried to find work. Her beauty, once a gift, became a curse. Prospective employers, instead of offering her jobs, offered inappropriate advances. Her life felt like a series of closed doors—until she met Ihfaaz.

Ihfaaz was different. Though he ran an illegal business, he was always respectful, always distant. At his office, she finally found a place where her beauty wasn't the focal point of her worth. Slowly, Nadia found herself drawn to the quiet sadness in his eyes—the same kind of sadness she carried within herself after her mother's death. She didn't know what had wounded Ihfaaz so deeply, but she wanted to be the one to heal him.

When her father's health began to decline from years of heavy drinking, Ihfaaz stepped in, helping to arrange for doctors and treatments. But nothing could reverse the damage. Her father passed away, leaving her alone in the world. Despite pressure from her relatives, Nadia chose not to move in with them. She wanted to be independent and moved into the working women's hostel instead, throwing herself fully into her work at Ihfaaz's office.

As her feelings for Ihfaaz deepened, Nadia wrestled with whether or not to tell him. She sensed that he cared for her in some way, even if he kept a distance. One night, unable to hold back any longer, she approached him in the quiet of the office. Her heart raced as she blurted out her confession, her voice trembling as she said, "Ihfaaz, I love you."

For a moment, silence filled the room. Ihfaaz, who had been focused on paperwork, leaned back in his chair and looked at her. His face remained calm, almost unreadable.

"Nadia," he said softly, "I can't love you back."

The words stung more than she expected. Her throat tightened, and she fought to keep the tears from spilling over. "Why?" she asked, her voice cracking. "What's wrong with me?"

Ihfaaz shook his head. "There's nothing wrong with you," he said, his tone gentle. "You're perfect. But I've lost the ability to love. There's nothing left inside me but emptiness."

Nadia wanted to scream, to argue with him, but the sorrow in his voice stopped her. She had seen that sadness in his eyes before, but hearing it now only confirmed what she had always suspected—something had broken Ihfaaz long ago, leaving him unable to give her the love she craved.

The next day, Nadia didn't come to work. But on the third day, she returned, her head held high. If Ihfaaz couldn't love her now, she would prove herself indispensable in other ways. She threw herself into the business, taking on more responsibility and managing key operations with the grace and strength her mother had once shown. Despite her heartache, she remained determined to stay by Ihfaaz's side, hoping that one day, she could heal the wounds he refused to acknowledge.

When Ihfaaz decided to move his operations to Sultanabad, Nadia followed without question. She had become an integral part of his empire, and there was no turning back. Sultanabad was new territory, a place filled with risk and opportunity, but Nadia didn't care. She was there for Ihfaaz, whether he knew it or not.

Chapter 27

N.E.S.T.

In the labyrinth of Indian government ministries, where power often moved in whispers and shadows, one organization stood as the most guarded secret. This organization was known as **N.E.S.T.** — the **National Espionage and Security Taskforce**, a covert force created to protect the nation from threats both within and beyond its borders, by any means necessary.

Established in the early 1970s, during a time of geopolitical upheaval and domestic instability, N.E.S.T. was born out of a necessity to operate beyond the purview of public agencies. Traditional intelligence services, tied down by bureaucracy and legal constraints, couldn't always act in real-time or with the required decisiveness. The government needed a force that could navigate the grey areas of espionage, intelligence gathering, and covert operations — all without leaving a trail.

N.E.S.T. was built to be deep and invisible. Even among the highest officials, only a select few knew of its existence. Its agents were carefully selected and placed within various government departments, ministries, and public offices. They served dual roles: one as ordinary public servants, and the other as operatives of N.E.S.T., reporting directly to the task force's leadership and carrying out missions that no one else could know about.

For over four decades, N.E.S.T. had operated in the shadows, with unlimited funding and the ability to influence anyone in the system, from local bureaucrats to senior officials. It handled both routine surveillance and highly sensitive missions, many of which were off-the-books, never to be officially acknowledged. Their reach extended into every corner of the country, and their authority was matched only by their discretion.

But now, they faced a new set of challenges, one that even their vast resources couldn't easily handle.

The room was dimly lit, with thick curtains drawn over the windows to keep prying eyes away. Around a long table sat the top officers of N.E.S.T., each placed strategically in high-level government roles, yet all part of the covert machine that was the National Espionage and Security Taskforce. At the head of the table sat Director Arun Kumar Singh, the stoic and calculating leader of N.E.S.T., a man who had seen the organization through numerous crises over the years.

Arun Kumar Singh, who had covertly worked at Kushalgram as officer at Bureau of Cross-Border Trade Compliance and Integrity, had been at the helm for over a decade, and under his leadership, N.E.S.T. had quietly expanded its influence, embedding its operatives deeper into the structures of government. With his steel-grey hair and calm demeanour, Singh commanded the room with little more than a look. Today, however, the challenge before them was one that even he found difficult to ignore.

"We have a serious problem on our hands," Singh began, his voice low but authoritative. "The number of ordinary Indian citizens being recruited by foreign intelligence agencies is growing. They're selling sensitive information for money, and the worst part is, these aren't your usual suspects. They're normal citizens — teachers, IT workers, even mid-level government employees. They're being lured by easy cash, and we're having a hard time keeping track of them."

Colonel Aditya Malhotra, one of the senior officers, leaned forward, his brow furrowed. "These people don't have the same motivations as traditional spies. They don't see themselves as traitors; they just see an opportunity to make money. The foreign agencies use them on use and throw basis, just for one or two recons or passing of information max.

After that they move on to recruit someone else. This decentralized, civilian espionage is becoming harder to detect and harder to control. We need a new strategy."

Shalini Rao, the head of counterintelligence, nodded in agreement. "The foreign agencies are smart. They're using money as bait, and they're doing it in a way that's completely off our radar. These civilians are flying under the intelligence community's radar, and by the time we catch them, the damage is already done."

Singh's expression darkened. "Which brings us to our second problem. Our own agents — the ones out in the field, conducting our most sensitive missions — are struggling to get the funds they need. We can't funnel money to them through official channels because these are off-the-books missions. But without cash, we're hamstrung. We need a way to support our agents without drawing any attention to ourselves."

The room fell silent as the gravity of the situation set in.

Vikram Naidu, N.E.S.T.'s financial expert, cleared his throat. "Director, we've been running into problems with our traditional methods of cash transfers. Banking systems are more tightly regulated than ever. Every large transaction is flagged, and moving cash across the country discreetly is becoming nearly impossible."

Singh nodded. "That's why we need an alternative. We can't continue relying on the same methods. We need a way to move large sums of money under the radar, without triggering any alarms."

Vikram hesitated for a moment before speaking again. "There is one option we haven't fully explored yet, but it's risky."

"Go on," Singh prompted.

"Hawala," Vikram said, letting the word hang in the air. "It's an informal money transfer system that operates completely outside the regulated banking channels. It's old, deeply entrenched, and almost impossible to trace. The key is trust between the hawala agents. If we can gain access to the right network, we can move money anywhere in the world without leaving a trail."

Shalini looked sceptical. "Hawala? Isn't that mostly used by smugglers and criminals?"

Vikram nodded. "Exactly. Which is why it's perfect for us. It's off the books, decentralized, and operates on trust. No paperwork, no digital footprint. But we need someone with the right connections to help us navigate that world."

Singh leaned back in his chair, his fingers steepled. "Who do you have in mind?"

Vikram replied. "Ihfaaz – He runs one of the largest and most discreet hawala networks in Mumbai. He's been flying under the radar for years, and from what we know, he's extremely cautious. His network could be exactly what we need to solve our cash flow problem."

Colonel Malhotra raised an eyebrow. "Can we trust him?"

Singh gave a small smile. "In our world, trust isn't the issue. It's leverage. Ihfaaz isn't a patriot, but he would surely value survival, and if he's smart and if we approach him the right way, he'll see the benefit of working with us. We have resources and influence that even he would find difficult to ignore."

The room was quiet as Singh's words sunk in. Everyone understood what this meant. N.E.S.T. was about to enter a new phase, one that required stepping even deeper into the shadows.

"Shalini, Vikram — you'll take the lead on this," Singh said, rising from his seat. "Reach out to Ihfaaz, carefully. We need to see if we can bring him into the fold. If we can secure his cooperation, we'll have the funds and the network we need to keep our agents in play, and to deal with the growing menace of civilian espionage."

The officers nodded, the plan now set into motion. N.E.S.T. had faced many challenges over the years, but this one was different. As they prepared to engage with the world of underground money flows and shadowy networks, one thing was clear — N.E.S.T. would do whatever it took to remain India's most powerful and secretive weapon. And with Ihfaaz's hawala network, they were about to find the solution to their most pressing problems.

After Ihfaaz's sudden shift to Sultanabad, N.E.S.T. officers faced a dilemma. The man who had operated so smoothly in Mumbai had now slipped out of their immediate reach. Sultanabad was a city cloaked in mystery and danger, where any misstep could mean exposing their carefully laid plans. Ihfaaz had unknowingly been under continuous surveillance, but the move disrupted their strategy. His sudden decision to sell his Mumbai home and stay primarily in hotels whenever he returned to the city complicated matters further.

The agents tasked with monitoring him found that Ihfaaz was rarely ever alone, regardless of whether he was in Mumbai or Sultanabad. His associates and staff were always nearby, creating a barrier that made discreet contact nearly impossible. Approaching him in Sultanabad, especially at his residence, was ruled out after much deliberation. His house there was an unknown entity. There was no telling what lay in store within its walls, and they couldn't afford any mistakes.

However, when Ihfaaz travelled to Mumbai, he stayed at hotels — his choice of accommodation more practical than luxurious, but always offering privacy and comfort. This provided the opportunity they were waiting for. After some research, the team discovered his preference for Seaview Heights, a 3-star hotel in Mumbai's Worli Sea Face area. The hotel was spacious, with a serene view of the Arabian Sea from its higher floors, offering Ihfaaz both quiet and discretion during his visits. The hotel's blend of anonymity and open spaces made it the perfect location for N.E.S.T. to finally make their move.

The officers crafted a plan to approach Ihfaaz in this setting, where the public yet private atmosphere of the hotel worked in their favour. They carefully timed their operation for his next visit, knowing that

Ihfaaz's movements would always be unpredictable, but his choice of hotel remained consistent.

Now, the question was not just how they would approach him but how to do so without arousing suspicion. Every detail had to be meticulously planned. One wrong step, and the whole operation could fall apart before it even began.

The night was quiet as Ihfaaz left Dinu Kaka's family home after a warm dinner. The streets of Mumbai, alive with their usual bustle, didn't register in his mind as he headed back to **Seaview Heights**. His day had been long, filled with meetings and planning for the future, but he felt content. The hotel's calming sea view and isolation were the perfect end to the night.

As he exited the elevator on his floor and walked down the dimly lit hallway toward his room, two figures suddenly emerged beside him. He turned slightly to his left, then his right, just as one of them spoke softly.

"Ihfaaz ji, we would like to have a word with you," said one of the men in a calm, measured voice. Before he could react, the cold steel of a pistol pressed against both his sides. It was a subtle but firm warning. Any sudden movement, and the conversation could take a dangerous turn.

"Get inside the room," the other officer added, his tone low but unmistakably authoritative. "Cooperate, and you'll have no problems. We just want to talk."

Ihfaaz's heart pounded, but he remained outwardly calm. There was no use resisting now; he would have to see what these people wanted. He opened the door and stepped into the hotel room. It was spacious, dimly lit, with the sound of distant waves crashing against the Worli shore faintly in the background.

As they entered, the two officers flanked him closely. Behind them, two more individuals, a man and a woman, entered the room — **Shalini** and **Vikram**, the senior officers of N.E.S.T. tasked with handling Ihfaaz. They moved with precision, locking the door behind them before silently motioning for him to sit down in the chair by the window.

Guns remained pointed at Ihfaaz as he took his seat. He was cornered, and escape was impossible. For a moment, no one spoke. The tension in the room was palpable, the silence suffocating. Ihfaaz's eyes moved between his captors, calculating his options. He knew better than to make any sudden moves.

Shalini and Vikram exchanged a brief glance before Vikram, standing to Ihfaaz's right, spoke first, his voice calm but with a slight edge.

"You've been under our watch for a long time, Mr. Ihfaaz. Now, we finally get to speak face to face."

Shalini stood just behind Vikram, her expression unreadable. She held her gun firmly, keeping it trained on Ihfaaz while listening intently.

"We're not here to harm you, but make no mistake," Vikram continued, "whether you walk out of here unscathed depends entirely on you."

The statement hung in the air, heavy with implied threats. Ihfaaz, though outwardly composed, could feel the weight of the situation. This wasn't a random attack or robbery. These people were professionals, and they wanted something important.

"What do you want?" Ihfaaz asked, his voice calm, though his mind raced.

"We'll get to that," Shalini interjected. "But first, let's make one thing clear. You're in no position to negotiate."

The room remained still, the atmosphere thick with unease. Whatever this conversation was about, it was going to change everything.

Ihfaaz's eyes, cold and sharp, scanned each of the four operatives standing before him. His mind was racing, but outwardly he exuded an unsettling calm. He spoke, his voice low but filled with icy defiance.

"Okay, fine," he said, locking eyes with Vikram. "If this is how you wish to proceed with our dialogue, then fire those guns and kill me. Because no matter what you do, you won't get me to do your bidding with this attitude of yours. And let me warn you — the more you threaten or torture me, the more difficult it'll be to extract whatever it is you want."

There was no fear in his tone, only a confidence that immediately shifted the dynamic in the room. Ihfaaz knew these weren't ordinary thugs. These people were professionals, but what he also knew was that they didn't seem to have any real leverage over him — at least not yet. He had built his world on calculated risks, and the scenario in front of him was just another gamble, one he was willing to play.

Vikram, reading the situation quickly, recognized that this man wasn't like the others they'd coerced before. Ihfaaz wasn't easily intimidated by threats or the prospect of violence. He glanced towards Shalini, who kept her stance firm, and then back to Ihfaaz, taking a breath to recalibrate his approach. It was clear their initial plan wasn't going to work.

"Let's not get hasty here," Vikram said, softening his tone, trying to introduce a more reasonable path. "We just need to discuss something. There's no need for violence."

Ihfaaz, sensing that the tide was turning, leaned back in his chair, his cold stare still fixed on Vikram. "Don't try to play good cop, bad cop with me," he retorted. "Shoot me, or get out of this room. I'm not having any sort of discussion with gun-wielding clowns."

The officer nearest to Ihfaaz, clearly less experienced and losing control of his patience, snapped. His fist slammed into Ihfaaz's stomach with force. Ihfaaz grunted but didn't break. Instead, he smirked, his lip curling up as he slowly lifted his head, eyes filled with steely defiance.

"Do whatever you need to do," he said with a grim satisfaction, catching his breath. "But I'm not talking with you. Get your boss here. Maybe he'll have more sense than you."

The room was still again. Vikram clenched his jaw, feeling the tension rise. They were on the edge of losing control of the entire situation, and that punch had just given Ihfaaz exactly what he wanted — proof that they didn't have the upper hand. Shalini's eyes flicked to Vikram, awaiting his next move. Both knew they needed to change tactics and fast.

Ihfaaz, on the other hand, sat comfortably, like a man who had just won the first round of a very dangerous game.

Vikram exchanged a look with Shalini, recognizing they had made a crucial error. Without a word, they holstered their guns and quietly left the room, closing the door behind them. Once outside, they walked down the dimly lit corridor and stopped near a window that overlooked the Mumbai skyline. The city lights sparkled in the distance, but the tension between them was thick.

"We need to fix this," Shalini said, her voice laced with frustration. "This isn't some low-level thug. Ihfaaz knows exactly how to push back, and we underestimated him."

Vikram nodded, still processing what had just happened. "We can't afford to make another misstep. We should brief the director and seek his guidance before things spiral further."

They quickly made their way to a secure location within the hotel, away from prying eyes. Using a secure line, they contacted Arun Singh, the director of NEST, who had been overseeing the entire operation from the shadows. The briefing was quick but detailed, explaining the situation — how Ihfaaz had called their bluff and turned the tables on them.

When the director finally spoke, his tone was sharp, laced with disappointment. "You two were supposed to be my best officers," he began, his voice a controlled growl. "You've had more than a month to orchestrate this, and you cornered him at the perfect moment. A neutral ground, away from his strongholds — and you let it slip. He's no fool. Now, he'll be alert, and that window of opportunity is gone. He'll be more cautious than ever, and we can't afford that."

Shalini and Vikram listened in silence, knowing that any excuse would only make things worse. The director was right — Ihfaaz would now be on guard, carefully planning his movements and the places he stayed.

Arun Singh took a deep breath before continuing. "Listen to me carefully," he said, his tone now more calculated. "Do not, under any circumstances, escalate the situation further. You've already done enough damage. Wait there. I'm coming down myself. If there's any chance to salvage this, I'll handle it."

The line went dead, leaving both officers standing in silence. Shalini looked over at Vikram, the weight of the director's words heavy on both of them.

"He's furious," Shalini muttered, her fingers tapping nervously against her side. "If we mess this up again, it won't just be Ihfaaz we'll have to worry about."

Vikram nodded, his face grim. "We need to step back and let him handle it. The director's the only one who can pull this off now. We wait."

As they returned to their positions near Ihfaaz's room, they kept their distance, both knowing that any further misstep would not only ruin the mission but possibly their careers as well.

As Vikram and Shalini re-entered the room, Ihfaaz was still seated in the chair, his eyes calm but sharp, sizing them up. Before they could speak, Ihfaaz raised an eyebrow and asked, "Do I have permission to have a glass of water and maybe a cigarette?"

Vikram, trying to maintain composure after the earlier confrontation, replied, "You're not a prisoner or a hostage, Ihfaaz ji."

One of the guards, standing near the minibar, grabbed a small bottle of water and handed it to Ihfaaz. With deliberate slowness, Ihfaaz opened the bottle, took a small sip, and then paused, holding the bottle at eye level. For a brief moment, everyone in the room tensed, unsure of his next move. Their eyes flicked to the bottle, thinking it might be used as a weapon. But instead of making any sudden moves, Ihfaaz calmly read aloud, "MRP: 15 rupees. And now they'll charge me 50 for this." He shook his head with a mock sigh. "There's a perfectly fine jug of water sitting on the table. You could've just given me that. Now you've burdened a poor man with an exorbitant expense of 50 rupees."

There was a flicker of irritation on Vikram's face, but he remained quiet. Both he and Shalini were experienced enough to understand that Ihfaaz was playing mind games, using these small provocations to establish psychological dominance over them. This was no ordinary man; he was testing them, poking at their professionalism with his casual attitude.

Ihfaaz then reached into his pocket, pulling out a pack of cigarettes. He offered one to Vikram, Shalini, and the two officers standing on either side of him, all the while maintaining a casual, almost friendly tone. "Smoke?" he asked.

They all politely declined, their eyes never leaving him. He smiled slightly, took one for himself, and lit it with a lighter. One of the officers moved to the balcony and opened the door, ensuring that the smoke wouldn't trigger the fire alarm. They all knew the game Ihfaaz was playing—stretching time, creating tension, and keeping them guessing.

For the next ten minutes, there was complete silence in the room. Ihfaaz sat calmly in the chair, taking long, slow drags from his cigarette, his face unreadable. The officers, including Vikram and Shalini, stood still, each feeling the weight of the silence. This wasn't how the confrontation was supposed to go, and everyone knew it.

After finishing his cigarette, Ihfaaz stubbed it out in the ashtray, exhaling the last puff of smoke. Another few moments passed, and still, no one spoke. Vikram and Shalini exchanged glances, realizing that Ihfaaz hadn't once asked why they were there, nor had he asked them to leave. He was completely in control of the moment, forcing them to make the first move.

Vikram felt the pressure mounting. This wasn't the reaction they had anticipated, and now, they were caught in a battle of wits with a man who was more than comfortable in these tense, high-stakes situations. Every second that passed felt like Ihfaaz was tightening his grip on the upper hand.

Finally, Ihfaaz leaned back in his chair and looked at them, his expression inscrutable. He had fully grasped the gravity of the situation. Either he had maneuvered himself into a position of psychological dominance, or this might be the last cigarette he ever smoked.

The tension in the room was palpable, the air thick with unspoken threats and possibilities. They all waited for someone to break the silence, but in that moment, Ihfaaz was in control—and he knew it.

Vikram's phone buzzed, breaking the stillness that had settled over the room. He answered it briefly and then walked to the door, unlocking it with a swift motion.

Arun Kumar Singh entered the room, his presence immediately shifting the atmosphere. Ihfaaz's eyes registered a flicker of surprise, but he masked it behind his usual calm face. Here was a man who had once worked at the Bureau of Cross-Border Trade Compliance and Integrity, someone Ihfaaz had crossed paths with in his former life, long before his reinvention. The last time they'd seen each other was 12 years ago, at his engagement to Varda—back when he was still Ahsan Faraz Khan.

A surge of questions filled Ihfaaz's mind. *What is Arun Singh doing here?* His thoughts spiralled as he considered a terrifying possibility: *Had his father discovered his survival and sent Arun Singh to bring him back? Had the carefully constructed web of deceit unravelled after all these years?* The idea made him uneasy, though he kept his emotions in check.

It had been more than a decade since that time, and Ihfaaz's appearance had changed drastically. There was little chance Singh would recognize him now.

As Arun Singh moved closer, Ihfaaz maintained a neutral expression, refusing to give anything away. Singh didn't immediately speak, taking a few steps forward and observing Ihfaaz with the same calm detachment Ihfaaz himself was displaying. The tension in the room thickened, a silent battle of wills playing out in the few feet of space between them.

As Arun Kumar Singh stepped into the room, he sniffed the air and wrinkled his nose slightly. "Who's been smoking in here?" he asked, his voice cutting through the tense silence.

Vikram quickly glanced at Ihfaaz.

Singh turned towards Ihfaaz, raising an eyebrow. "Young man, that's a pretty bad habit for someone your age and health," he remarked with a faint smirk.

Ihfaaz responded with a calm, knowing smile but said nothing.

Arun Singh then addressed his team. "Lower your weapons. Are you people idiots? We're here to have a chat, not point guns at him."

The officers hesitated, then slowly put their guns away, casting uneasy glances at each other. Singh shook his head in quiet frustration and turned back to Ihfaaz.

"I apologize for their behaviour," he said, his voice smoother now. "Let's step outside for a moment."

He gestured toward the balcony. Ihfaaz gave a small nod and followed him outside. The cool breeze from the sea provided a momentary relief from the thick tension inside the room.

Leaning against the balcony railing, Arun Singh spoke plainly but carefully. "I'll get straight to the point. We're part of an organization that operates quietly, very quietly. You're a smart man; I'm sure you can guess the kind of work we do."

Ihfaaz listened intently, his expression unreadable.

"We need your help, Ihfaaz," Singh continued, lowering his voice. "There's been an increasing flow of money being funnelled to ordinary citizens—people who are unknowingly being used to carry out espionage for foreign powers. We need a way to track and control that flow, and... we also need funds for certain missions that aren't exactly in the books."

He paused, letting the gravity of his words sink in. "Now, we don't care about your hawala business, not directly. But if you help us, we're willing to help you in the future. Of course, there are boundaries. No drugs, no anti-national activities. But... other things can be discussed, depending on the situation."

Arun Singh gave a small, calculating smile. "Rest assured, your cooperation won't go unnoticed."

Ihfaaz, still silent, processed the offer carefully. His mind raced through the implications, though his expression gave nothing away.

Ihfaaz stood silent for a moment, his eyes drifting toward the dark sea beyond the balcony. The crashing waves mirrored the turbulence in his mind. After a long pause, he gave a small, contemplative "Hmm..." before speaking.

"If I cooperate with you," Ihfaaz began, his voice calm but with a subtle edge, "then clearly, I would be cheating on my clients, my partners. I'm sure you know how complex my business is. It's built on trust, a fragile one at that."

Arun Singh didn't miss a beat. "Yes, we know. You operate as an unofficial central bank for the hawala business. Correct me if I'm wrong, but we estimate around 60 to 70 percent of the hawala money circulating through the country flows through your system."

Ihfaaz tilted his head slightly but didn't refute the claim.

"We don't care about the methods you use," Singh continued. "But yes, revealing the source would be a betrayal. However, if we keep your role a secret, there's nothing for you to lose. You can continue business as usual. No one needs to know."

Ihfaaz exhaled slowly, weighing the proposition in his head. "And if I decline?"

Arun Singh's expression shifted slightly, a hint of a smile playing on his lips. "Ihfaaz, you must understand that we're an organization with access to every department within the government. No matter how many people are on your payroll or how many investors are tied to your operation, they won't be able to help you. We wouldn't harm you physically; that's not our style."

He leaned in slightly, his voice lowering. "But we can use our resources to shut you down. We can ensure that your entire business collapses, and if needed, we can even prop up your competitors, building a replica of your operation. You'd be left with nothing."

The words hung in the air, not as a threat, but a cold, calculated fact.

"However," Singh continued, his tone now more diplomatic, "from everything we've heard, you're an intelligent man. Known to make sound decisions. This is one of those moments where a wise choice could save you a lot of trouble."

Ihfaaz remained silent, his mind racing. He was keenly aware of the weight of the situation. If he agreed, he could maintain his empire in secret. If he declined, his carefully built empire could crumble. The question was: how far could he trust them to keep their end of the deal?

As they stood on the balcony, the tension shifted slightly. Ihfaaz offered Arun Singh a cup of coffee. This momentarily diffused the earlier hostility. Arun Singh took the gesture as a sign that perhaps Ihfaaz was willing to engage more seriously. After calling room service and ordering six cups, the wait for coffee stretched out in silence, with both men lost in their thoughts. Ihfaaz's mind raced, plotting his next move while maintaining an air of calm.

When the coffee finally arrived, the two men resumed their place on the balcony while Vikram, Shalini, and the others stayed inside. Ihfaaz casually closed the door connecting the balcony and the room and sipping his cup slowly, Ihfaaz gauged the situation. He leaned slightly closer to Arun, ensuring their conversation wouldn't be overheard.

"By the way," Ihfaaz began casually, "what exactly is the name of this organization you're working with? Is it the Bureau of Cross-Border Trade Compliance and Integrity, or something else entirely?"

Arun Singh was visibly taken aback by the question. It was unexpected, a clear sign that Ihfaaz knew more than he was letting on. However, years of field experience allowed Arun to mask his surprise. With a calm, measured tone, he responded, "Sure, it could be that, especially if we were based around the Bangladesh or Nepal border."

Ihfaaz smirked, taking another sip of his coffee. "Interesting. From what I remember, the Bureau of Cross-Border Trade Compliance and Integrity was never in the business of wielding guns or abducting civilians. But then again," he paused, letting the words hang in the air, "times do change, don't they?"

Arun Singh's mind was now racing, trying to place this man. Something about him, his confidence, his knowledge—there was a familiarity there. And then it clicked. Memories from years ago resurfaced, memories from a different life, different circumstances. His face barely shifted, but the realization was clear in his eyes.

"Yes," Arun Singh replied quietly, his voice laced with sudden recognition. "Times do change. So do people… and so do names. Isn't that right, Ahsan?"

Arun Singh leaned back slightly, a small smirk playing on his lips as he continued, "The last time we met, you were very lean, had those long, stylish hair with a beard, and you were on cloud nine—engaged to the love of your life. Now, look at you. Faking your own death, built like a soldier with that crew cut, clean-shaven face, and deeply involved in illegal hawala and God knows what sort of activities. Smoking cigarettes while your family still mourns your death, especially my dear friend Faraz."

Ihfaaz looked up slowly, his empty, cold eyes locking onto Arun's with a steely glare. His voice was flat, devoid of emotion. "Yes, your dear friend Faraz—the one who left me when I needed him the most. Who wouldn't even listen to me, wouldn't hear my side of the story." He paused, the bitterness creeping into his voice. "And my brothers, more concerned about their egos and the business than about their own blood. Some family I had."

The atmosphere between them thickened, charged with unspoken histories and buried resentments. Ihfaaz's anger, though controlled, simmered just beneath the surface, each word cutting deeper into the past he had tried to escape.

"You see, Sir, I didn't have the luxury of family support. When Varda's father twisted the story, I was already condemned in their eyes. And when I needed them the most, they were nowhere to be found." His gaze hardened, a mixture of fury and pain flickering briefly in his expression. "I did what I had to. I became someone else. Ahsan died that day."

Arun Singh, though seasoned in his line of work, couldn't ignore the deep-seated emotions behind Ihfaaz's words. He chose not to respond immediately, letting the weight of what had been said settle.

"You're right," Arun finally said, softer than before. "It was a mess. But you know Faraz... he's not the man who abandoned you out of cruelty. He's grieving—his heart still holds onto Ahsan, his son, not this man in front of me."

Ihfaaz gave a cold, mirthless chuckle. "That man, Ahsan, is dead. This man, Ihfaaz, has other plans now."

Ihfaaz's eyes remained cold and calculating as he continued. "The question now is, what can Arun Kumar Singh and his organization offer to Ihfaaz Ahmed Khan in return for his services? And not just that—consider that Ihfaaz Ahmed Khan has a penchant for power. You have no idea how much you stand to gain if you join hands with me. The benefits would be manifold compared to what you used to gain during those long closed-door meetings with your Faraz Khan."

Arun Singh raised an eyebrow, intrigued. Ihfaaz continued, "Yes, I know Mr. Faraz Khan used to share a lot of intelligence and smuggling-related details with you. I might have overheard a few things. That's why he had a free hand to smuggle non-invasive products. I don't need an immediate answer. I'm ready to cooperate in every possible way. But first, I need a promise: keep my past a secret—from your organization, your family, and above all, my own family. If I get any hint that my previous life is exposed, our deal is off. Even if it means you have to imprison me or worse."

Arun Singh took in Ihfaaz's words, the bitterness and determination evident in his tone. Instead of reacting with anger, Arun Singh felt a twinge of sympathy for the man before him. He nodded, extending his hand towards Ihfaaz. "We have a deal."

They shook hands, sealing their agreement. Both men entered the room, where Shalini, Vikram, and the two junior officers waited anxiously. The officers had been watching through the glass partition but had been unable to hear the conversation.

When they saw the handshake, they realized that the situation had been resolved. Arun Singh introduced Vikram and Shalini to Ihfaaz, acknowledging the successful negotiation.

"We've achieved more than we had planned," Arun Singh informed his team. "We will discuss the modus operandi of this new partnership in further detail in our next meeting."

Chapter 28

The next day, Arun Singh, Vikram, and Shalini gathered again in Ihfaaz's hotel room. The atmosphere, while not entirely warm, was significantly more relaxed than their previous encounter. There was still an air of caution and scepticism lingering between both sides—none of them were quite ready to trust the other fully. Arun Singh, however, remained the linchpin of the conversation, deftly steering it away from personal matters, especially anything related to Kushalgram, which he purposely avoided in front of his officers.

As they sat down to discuss the practicalities, the meeting took on a more businesslike tone. The details of how the money would be transferred to their field agents were meticulously worked out. Ihfaaz, always a step ahead, proposed a solution that caught their attention: the use of ATM cards for discreet withdrawals. Arun, Vikram, and Shalini were immediately on board with the idea, recognizing the simplicity and anonymity it offered.

Still, one major issue loomed over them—the identification of the espionage network. Half of their concerns had been alleviated by the structure Ihfaaz proposed for the financial transfers, but the other half, identifying the individuals involved in espionage, remained unresolved.

"ATM cards are a good start," Arun acknowledged, "but we need a way to trace the money back to those conducting espionage, without them realizing they're being monitored."

Ihfaaz nodded thoughtfully, leaning back in his chair. "I can provide you with the funds and ensure the anonymity of your agents. But if you want to expose those running the espionage network, we'll need more than just finances—we'll need information. Something to bait them into revealing themselves."

Vikram looked to Shalini, who was scribbling down notes, and then back to Arun Singh. "It's a start," he agreed. "We'll need to brainstorm more together to crack this. But if we can trust this system, we've already cleared a significant hurdle."

Arun Singh remained neutral, watching both sides carefully, ensuring no one overstepped. "We're in this together for now, but remember—we have to tread carefully. We're walking a fine line."

The meeting ended on that cautious note, with plans to meet again soon, as they knew their alliance was fragile, but with the potential for mutual benefit if played correctly. The dance of cooperation and suspicion would continue.

A couple of days later, Vikram was in a deep sleep at around 3 a.m. when his phone rang. Startled, he groggily checked the caller ID, and to his surprise, it was Ihfaaz. The flashing name on the screen filled Vikram with a sense of dread, assuming that Ihfaaz must have gotten himself into trouble and was about to cash in on his bargaining chip with NEST to get out of it.

Irritated, Vikram answered the phone, his voice thick with sleep. "It's 3 a.m., Ihfaaz. This better be good."

On the other end, Ihfaaz's voice was sharp, cutting through the silence. "I know. I have a watch too, and it works just fine," he replied curtly. "Tell me, Vikram, how many people have you arrested on suspicion in the last 12 months?"

Vikram blinked, confused. What sort of question was that? And why at this ungodly hour? He rubbed his eyes, trying to make sense of the odd inquiry. "Uh... maybe around 25 to 30. Why?"

"Great," Ihfaaz replied with chilling precision. "I need you to do something for me. Question every single one of them. Ask them the exact date they received the money through the hawala channel, the agent's name, location, and the amount. Make sure the dates align. Collect all the data and send it to me."

Before Vikram could even react, Ihfaaz disconnected the call abruptly—no thanks, no explanation, no goodbye.

Vikram and his team delivered as expected. Over the following week, they worked diligently to track down the 28 individuals who had been arrested on suspicion during the last 12 months, spread across various jails in different parts of the country. Each one of them was interrogated again, this time with the specific focus on the details Ihfaaz had requested: the exact date they received the money through the hawala channel, the agent's name, location, and the amount.

It was a painstaking process, requiring coordination between multiple regions and law enforcement divisions, but Vikram ensured that every angle was covered. Slowly but surely, the data came together—every piece of information meticulously recorded, cross-verified, and then sent to Ihfaaz. A week later, the full dossier of information landed in Ihfaaz's hands.

The question that lingered with Vikram, however, was what exactly Ihfaaz intended to do with this data. He knew better than to ask, but the curiosity gnawed at him. Ihfaaz always had a plan, but this one seemed more intricate and layered than the usual operations.

A fortnight had passed since Ihfaaz had been given the data, and now it was time for another crucial meeting. Arun Singh, Shalini, and Vikram met with him again at the same hotel in Mumbai, all of them uncertain yet intrigued about what the outcome of Ihfaaz's deep dive into the hawala network would be.

As they gathered in the room, Ihfaaz, maintaining his composed demeanour, handed over a neatly prepared list to Arun Singh. The paper contained three names and their contact details—individuals who, based on the data Vikram's team had gathered, were the common link across all transactions. These were the key operatives who facilitated the movement of funds, making them critical players in the espionage network.

For a moment, the room fell into silence as the team from N.E.S.T. processed the information. Though they maintained their professional detachment, the energy shifted. Internally, they were elated. If Ihfaaz's information was accurate, this could be the breakthrough they had been hunting for over two years, finally placing them in a position to dismantle the source of the clandestine funding.

Arun Singh glanced at the list, then back at Ihfaaz. "If these names lead where we think they do," he said slowly, "you've just given us the key to unravelling the entire operation."

Ihfaaz remained impassive. "I've done my part. Now, it's up to you to act on it."

Vikram and Shalini exchanged glances. They knew how significant this moment was. What had eluded them for the past 24 months was now in their grasp—thanks to the very man they had initially approached with caution and suspicion. The balance of power in this relationship was shifting, and they were fully aware of it.

Arun Singh, ever the seasoned professional, remained calm. "We'll take it from here. But rest assured, your contribution won't be forgotten."

Chapter 29

Over the next three years, Ihfaaz's life unfolded smoothly, almost seamlessly. His business ventures thrived, with profits soaring to new heights. Relations with N.E.S.T. had evolved as well—while they weren't friendly, there was a mutual understanding and respect, a professional accord that allowed both sides to benefit from their association. The shell companies he had established flourished, providing a robust front for his operations, and over time, Ihfaaz intentionally distanced himself from the day-to-day handling of the money laundering and hawala business.

His role had shifted. No longer the hands-on mastermind behind every transaction, Ihfaaz had assumed more of a supervisory position. His trusted staff, meticulously chosen and trained, had taken over the daily responsibilities. They ran the operations efficiently, ensuring everything moved like clockwork. Ihfaaz, meanwhile, had become more involved in higher-level business dealings—hearing pitches for new projects, making key investment decisions, and settling disputes, all while maintaining his discretion and staying under the radar.

It was a lifestyle that suited him—a careful balance of power, wealth, and influence, all without drawing unwanted attention. But then, the lull was disturbed. The calm shattered. An attempt was made on his life.

Was it a new enemy, someone rising from the shadows to claim his throne? Or was it N.E.S.T., the very organization that had benefited from his expertise, now deciding that he had outlived his usefulness? Had they exhausted all they could from him, and now sought to erase him from the equation? Or was it something else entirely—perhaps the past, creeping back with all its bitterness and unresolved wounds, coming to haunt him when he least expected it?

The questions hung in the air, unanswered. But one thing was clear—nothing in Ihfaaz's life would be the same again.

Chapter 30

Present Day

The sterile smell of the hospital was a harsh contrast to the chaos that had just unfolded. As the ambulance doors swung open, the team of doctors, ready and resolute, swiftly wheeled Ihfaaz into the building. Nadia, her face pale and streaked with tears, clung to Ihfaaz's side as they were ushered to the third floor.

In the dim light of the ambulance, she could see Ihfaaz's once strong and defiant features now weakened and pale. His grip on her hand was feeble, but it was the first time Nadia felt the warmth of his touch—a warmth that seemed to defy the gravity of the situation.

"Business as usual, tomorrow, whatever happens to me," he murmured, his voice barely a whisper but filled with an odd sense of calm. The weak smile on his lips was both a comfort and a heartbreaking farewell.

Tears flowed freely down Nadia's cheeks as she struggled to hold back her sobs. The ambulance had barely come to a halt before Ihfaaz was whisked away to the operating theatre. Nadia's tears had dried into a steely resolve. She knew what needed to be done.

As she wiped her tears, she noticed Ihfaaz's phone lying on the seat beside her. It was still on, its screen glowing with notifications. She took a deep breath, picked up her phone, and dialled Pradip's number.

"Pradip, it's Nadia. We've had an emergency. Ihfaaz has been shot. He's in surgery now. I need you to leave for Sultanabad immediately," she said, her voice steady despite the turmoil within.

Pradip's concerned voice came through the line, promising he'd be on his way. Nadia hung up and moved on to type a message on the office Whatsapp group, “There’s been an incident involving Ihfaaz Sir. He’s been shot and is currently in surgery. I need everyone to proceed with business as usual tomorrow. We’ll handle everything else from here,”

After the call and the Whatsapp message the immediate crisis was addressed, Nadia found a quiet corner in the hospital lobby. The reality of the situation was sinking in, but her mind remained focused on keeping the operation running smoothly in Ihfaaz’s absence. Her heart ached with uncertainty, but she knew that right now, there was no room for anything but resolve.

Time seemed to stretch infinitely as Nadia sat rigidly on the bench outside the operation theatre. Each glance at the door, each check of her mobile, only heightened the feeling that the world had paused, holding its breath along with her.

The severity of Ihfaaz’s condition weighed heavily on her. While the task of uncovering who was responsible for this would have to wait, her immediate focus was solely on his well-being. The hospital, being part of Ihfaaz’s syndicate, was efficient and responsive, handling all the necessary procedures without the usual bureaucratic hurdles. Nadia’s thoughts remained fixed on Ihfaaz.

A senior doctor, noting Nadia’s unwavering vigil, approached her. “Miss, please, you should sit in a nearby office. These surgeries can take quite a while.”

Nadia shook her head, her eyes never leaving the door. “I’ll stay here. I need to be here.”

The doctor, seeing her resolve, sighed and walked to the nearest nursing station. He picked up a phone and dialled a number. After a brief conversation, an orderly arrived with a tray. Coffee, biscuits, and a bottle of water were placed in front of Nadia.

"Please, you need to drink and eat something," the doctor insisted. "We're concerned you might go into shock if you don't."

Nadia accepted the coffee and biscuits with a reluctant nod. She sipped the coffee and ate the biscuits while maintaining her anxious watch on the operation theatre. The doctor's reassurances that Ihfaaz was in good hands were little comfort against the gnawing uncertainty she felt.

Just as she finished her coffee, the sudden commotion at the elevator drew her attention. The police team had arrived. Nadia's heart sank as she saw the newly appointed S.P., Abhishek, leading the group. His presence was unexpected and unwelcome; she had only heard scattered information about him and wasn't sure how he would handle this situation.

Dr. Patel, the senior doctor, leaned in and whispered, "We had to inform them. Please understand. The situation requires their attention."

Nadia nodded, though her concern was evident. Abhishek had recently taken over as Sultanabad's S.P., and while he was known for his integrity, she had yet to gauge how he would navigate this complex scenario.

As Abhishek entered the hospital, he headed straight towards Dr. Patel, ignoring Nadia completely. "We will need a statement from the hospital. Secondly, is there anyone with the victim?"

Dr. Patel glanced at Nadia and began to introduce her, but Abhishek cut him off. "You are?" he asked curtly.

Nadia, feeling the sharp edge in his tone, responded with equal bluntness, "I am Nadia D'Souza. I work with Mr. Ihfaaz."

Abhishek raised an eyebrow. "Hmm... Mr. Ihfaaz... and what exactly does your Mr. Ihfaaz do to end up in this condition?"

Nadia bristled at his implication but kept her composure. "Mr. Ihfaaz is an entrepreneur and involved in strategic investing."

Abhishek gave a dismissive nod. "We will see. I want no visitors and no unnecessary staff attending to the patient."

Dr. Patel nodded in agreement. "Sir, we have already vacated this part of the floor. Access has been restricted, and we will adhere to your orders."

"Great," Abhishek said. "I should be the first to speak with the patient when he regains consciousness." He glanced at Nadia. "No one else."

Turning to Nadia, he asked, "Did you witness the incident?"

Nadia shook her head. "No, I was in the office. When I heard the gunshots, I saw from the window and ran down."

Abhishek's expression hardened. "Why didn't you or someone from your office call the police? We need to secure the crime scene. God knows what evidence might have been contaminated by now."

Nadia's frustration boiled over. "I was more concerned about attending to Mr. Ihfaaz. It might have slipped my mind."

Abhishek's gaze was icy. "Hmm, slipped your mind, right? Fine. You need to leave. We or the hospital will let you know if there is anything to report."

Nadia's patience snapped. "No, I will not leave. I have every right to be here with, with ....."

"With what?" Abhishek interrupted, his tone dripping with scepticism.

Dr. Patel stepped in, trying to mediate. "Sir, she can wait in the nearby cabin. We will update her as soon as Mr. Ihfaaz regains consciousness."

Abhishek nodded curtly. "Alright."

Nadia, fuming with frustration, retreated to the nearby office. She swore under her breath, the weight of worry and anger mingling as she waited for any news about Ihfaaz.

After three long hours, the surgery was complete, and Ihfaaz was wheeled into the ICU. Nadia's heart raced as Abhishek was promptly informed and arrived at the scene. He spoke with Dr. Sharma, the lead surgeon, his face serious and focused.

Once their conversation concluded, Dr. Sharma approached Nadia. "Mr. Ihfaaz is safe and out of immediate danger," he assured her. "He's stable, though still quite pale. It may take him about four to five hours to regain consciousness. You can see him now."

Nadia's heart lifted with relief. She thanked Dr. Sharma and practically ran to the ICU. Inside, she found Ihfaaz lying in the bed, connected to various monitors and IV lines. He looked a bit pale and fragile, but the steady beep of the heart monitor and the gentle rise and fall of his chest assured her that he was alive and stable.

Tears welled in her eyes as she took in the sight of him, peacefully resting despite the ordeal. Nadia whispered a heartfelt prayer of gratitude to God. The sight of Ihfaaz in his deep slumber was both a comfort and a reminder of the long road ahead.

Returning to the nearby office, Nadia set herself up for what would be a long wait. No one was allowed on the floor except for essential staff, and she feared that if she left, she might not be allowed back in. She decided to stay put, staying in touch with everyone via phone.

Pradip was already on his way, deboarding from a flight at Nagpur airport and expected to arrive in four to five hours. Meanwhile, Nadia kept the office staff updated. They were relieved to hear that Ihfaaz was out of danger, though the anxiety of the situation was palpable.

Sitting alone in the office, Nadia pondered the years she had worked with Ihfaaz and the unanswered questions about his personal life. She had never been able to find any information about his relatives, and now, in the absence of any family to notify, it fell to her to manage everything.

As she waited, Nadia resolved that once Ihfaaz was back on his feet, things between them would change. The ordeal had made her realize the depth of her feelings and her commitment to seeing him through this crisis. Despite the uncertainty of the future, she knew that she would stand by him, no matter what.

As the hours ticked by, Nadia remained in the office, her mind drifting between worry and determination. Meanwhile, Abhishek's team worked diligently outside the hospital, but some of the subordinate officers were puzzled. They whispered among themselves, wondering why their superior, a high-ranking officer like S.P. Abhishek, was so personally involved in what seemed like a routine investigative matter.

Granted, the shooting of Ihfaaz was a significant and rare event in Sultanabad's history, but still, there were other capable officers who could have handled much of the legwork. The S.P. seemed to be overseeing every detail himself, which was unusual for someone in his position. His intense involvement raised eyebrows, though no one dared question him openly.

What Nadia didn't know was that the police had arrived at the scene of the attack mere minutes after the ambulance had left. They had received a call from someone informing about the attack. The attack on Ihfaaz had sparked a connection in Abhishek's mind — he was already trying to piece together how the shooting related to another mysterious incident from earlier in the day: the car explosion that had resulted in all the assassins being killed.

The blast, initially thought to be an isolated event, now seemed to intertwine with Ihfaaz's shooting. There were dots that Abhishek was trying to connect, a larger, more sinister plot at play, and this was no longer just about a high-profile businessman being targeted.

As the investigation unfolded, Abhishek's team gathered more evidence, working quietly but efficiently. The S.P.'s involvement hinted that this was bigger than it appeared on the surface, and the implications of the attack, paired with the earlier explosion, suggested a coordinated operation. The more the officers uncovered, the clearer it became that this was not just an ordinary crime, but a deep, calculated strike with broader implications.

Chapter 31

Arun Singh was preparing for bed when his phone rang. It was Vikram, his voice tense as he informed him about the attack on Ihfaaz. Arun listened to the full report without interrupting. After a moment, he asked quietly, "Did we do it?"

"No, sir, absolutely not," Vikram replied firmly. "We're not involved. Anything like this would have gone through you first."

"Hmmm..." Arun sighed, considering the situation. "Head to Sultanabad immediately. I'll be there by tomorrow. Meanwhile, gather as much intelligence as you can from the police. If you hit any roadblocks, call me. I'll speak to the IG myself."

Vikram affirmed his orders and ended the call.

Alone in his room, Arun sat in silence, staring at his phone. His mind raced. Should he call Faraz Khan?

Arun weighed his options carefully. He decided to wait. There was still too much uncertainty, and he needed more information before making any moves. He would wait until he had more clarity before deciding whether to inform Faraz Khan.

In the early hours of the morning, Ihfaaz finally regained consciousness. His eyelids fluttered, and a faint awareness began to return. The doctors attending to him quickly assessed his condition and immediately informed S.P. Abhishek. Within half an hour, Abhishek arrived at the hospital, his pace brisk as he moved toward the ICU.

Nadia, who had been waiting tirelessly for any news, had dozed off in one of the office cabins on the hospital floor. The doctors, aware of her exhaustion, decided not to disturb her yet. They thought it best for Abhishek to speak with Ihfaaz first, then they would wake Nadia.

Meanwhile, Pradip had already arrived in Sultanabad and checked into a hotel, staying in close contact with Nadia over the phone. Though no one was allowed inside the hospital, he remained on standby, waiting for any update about Ihfaaz's condition.

Abhishek entered the ICU with a sense of urgency, but his meeting with Ihfaaz was brief, lasting no more than five to seven minutes. He exited the room shortly after, his expression unreadable. The doctors advised that Ihfaaz needed rest and that further questioning could wait.

Once Abhishek left, one of the nurses gently shook Nadia awake. Groggy and confused, it took a moment for Nadia to realize what was happening. "Ihfaaz has woken up," the nurse informed her with a soft smile.

Nadia rushed to the ICU, her heart pounding in her chest. As she entered the room, she found Ihfaaz lying in his bed, pale and weak but very much alive. His eyes, though heavy with exhaustion, managed to focus on her, and a faint smile crept across his face. For the first time since the attack, Nadia felt a wave of relief wash over her. Ihfaaz was going to be okay.

He fell back into a deep sleep, still recovering, but Nadia's spirit was lifted. She stood by his side for a few moments longer, watching the steady rise and fall of his chest. Soon, he would regain his strength, and things would begin to return to normal.

Nadia left the ICU quietly, comforted by the knowledge that Ihfaaz had made it through the worst. Now, it was just a matter of time before he was fully back on his feet.

The doctors on duty advised her to go home and take some rest. They were there for him and any new development would be promptly informed to her over phone. Finally she agreed and left the hospital for her home. Reaching her home, she lied on the bed and immediately fell into deep sleep where all she could dream of was guns, bullets and blood.

Abhishek reached his office at 11 am sharp after having a good three hours' sleep. He had a lot of things to attend to apart from Ihfaaz and the car bombing. Just as he sat at his desk, an orderly came and put a chit in front of him with a name: Mr. Vikram from the Bureau of Cross-Border Trade Compliance and Integrity was waiting for him. He was puzzled as to what someone from that department would have to do with Sultanabad. He told the orderly to ask the person to wait a while and started working on the task at hand.

About half an hour later, he got a call from the D.I.G. office. He was asked to leave everything in hand and attend to Mr. Vikram. Abhishek's curiosity was piqued. He pressed the bell button and asked the orderly to let Mr. Vikram in.

When Mr. Vikram entered the office, Abhishek noticed his sharp expression and the briefcase he carried. "Mr. Vikram, please have a seat. I was instructed to prioritize our meeting. What brings you here?"

Vikram replied, "Sir, I would request your good selves to share with us all the case details that you have about last night's shooting incident on Mr. Ihfaaz."

Abhishek frowned a bit and replied, "I don't know who exactly you are and what it is in it for you or your department that you are interested in some random shooting attempt on a hawala operator."

Vikram responded, "With all due respect, I am not at liberty to disclose that to you, sir."

Abhishek, now a bit agitated, said, "Then even I am not at liberty to disclose the case and investigation details to someone outside my department's purview. I agreed to meet you just because someone from the D.I.G. office called me. Ask your department to approach us through official channels, and if I have written authorization from my superiors, then only will we meet. Thank you."

He motioned Vikram to leave. Vikram did not take it personally; he was used to such resistance. He left Abhishek's office and informed Arun Singh about the interaction. Arun Singh instructed him to stay put in Sultanabad as he would be arriving in the next 2 to 3 hours, and then they would address the matter together.

It was business as usual at Ihfaaz's offices. The day proceeded with its routine tasks, and the staff went about their work with a sense of normalcy. Despite the previous night's dramatic event, the atmosphere in the office was calm and controlled.

There were a number of concerned phone calls to Nadia, Pradip, and their subordinates, who were fielding inquiries about the shooting incident. They assured the callers that while Ihfaaz had indeed been shot, he was in stable condition and recuperating. The message was clear: Ihfaaz was resting and expected to return to work within a week or ten days.

This news was a relief to many. The fact that Ihfaaz was alive and that operations continued smoothly helped to soothe the anxious nerves of those involved. The reassurance that business was continuing as usual provided a sense of stability and normalcy, calming the worries that had surfaced in the wake of the shooting.

Abhishek was busy surveying what little remained of the car that had been destroyed in the blast. Pieces of charred metal and debris lay scattered around, and the air still carried the faint smell of burnt rubber. His phone buzzed. Glancing at the screen, he saw it was the D.I.G. calling. He quickly answered, straightening up as if the call demanded his full attention.

"Good morning, sir," Abhishek greeted after the usual pleasantries.

The D.I.G. didn't waste time. "Abhishek, what's the status of my instructions regarding cooperation with Vikram and his team?"

Abhishek hesitated for a brief moment before responding. "Sir, Vikram requested full details of the case investigation, but since I had no direct orders from you, I didn't share anything. I thought it best to hold off until you gave explicit instructions."

The D.I.G.'s tone sharpened. "Let me be clear, Abhishek. You are to comply with every request from Vikram and his team. If you need written orders, you'll get them within the next 30 minutes. Understood?"

Abhishek felt the weight of the situation sink in. He knew asking for written orders could complicate matters, and the D.I.G.'s stern tone left no room for argument. He responded quickly, "No sir, now that you've verbally ordered me, written orders aren't necessary."

"Good," the D.I.G. replied curtly. "Do you have Vikram's number?"

"No, sir," Abhishek answered.

"I'm sending it to you now. Vikram and his boss are at the Government Guest House. Go there and meet them," the D.I.G. instructed.

Hesitantly, Abhishek asked, "Sir, who exactly are these people, and why are we accommodating them so much?"

The D.I.G. paused for a moment, his voice softening slightly. "I don't know who they are exactly, Abhishek, but I've received explicit instructions from my superiors that they should have our full cooperation. From what I understand, their hierarchy is way above ours. So, let's focus on keeping them happy. Is that clear?"

"Yes, sir," Abhishek replied, the gravity of the situation becoming clearer.

As soon as he disconnected the call, he received Vikram's number via message. Wasting no time, he dialled.

The call was answered on the second ring. "Vikram here."

"Vikram, this is Abhishek, S.P. Sultanabad. I've been instructed to meet you."

"Ah, yes, Abhishek sir. My boss and I are currently at the Government Guest House, and he would like to meet you. How soon can you be here?"

"Give me 15 minutes, and I'll be there," Abhishek replied.

"Great," Vikram said, his voice noticeably pleased. "See you soon."

After ending the call, Vikram's grin widened. Arun Singh, seated beside him, noticed and asked, "Who's got you smiling like that? Someone special?"

"Indeed," Vikram replied. "The S.P. of Sultanabad is coming to meet us in 15 minutes."

Arun Singh leaned back, raising an eyebrow. "Then let's get ready for a long conversation with Mr. Abhishek, shall we?"

Vikram chuckled and nodded in agreement. "It's going to be an interesting meeting, no doubt."

Chapter 32

It took more than 15 minutes for Abhishek to reach the Government Guest House. As he stepped out of his car, the air was thick with the heat of the late afternoon sun. A pair of armed guards stood at attention near the entrance, nodding as Abhishek passed. He was directed by an attendant to a quiet corner room where Vikram was waiting.

"Abhishek ji, welcome," Vikram greeted him with a formal nod, his tone respectful but measured. He gestured toward the door. "Mr. Arun Kumar Singh is already inside. Please, follow me."

As they entered the room, Abhishek's eyes took in the setting. The guest house's room was modest but comfortable, with soft beige walls and sunlight filtering through heavy curtains. Arun Kumar Singh stood near a window, his posture relaxed yet commanding. His presence filled the space with a sense of quiet authority.

"Abhishek ji," Arun greeted him as he extended his hand. "I'm Arun Kumar Singh. It's good to finally meet you."

After exchanging pleasantries, Arun gestured toward the coffee table. "Please, have a seat. Would you like some coffee?"

"No, thank you, sir. I'm fine," Abhishek replied politely, his mind already focused on the task at hand.

Arun chuckled softly. "Come now, Abhishek ji. We have a lot to discuss. Let's have some coffee while we're at it."

There was something about Arun's manner—firm but affable—that made refusal feel out of place. Abhishek relented. "Alright then, coffee it is."

As the three men settled into their seats, coffee cups in hand, the mood in the room grew more serious. Vikram and Arun exchanged a brief glance, signalling they were ready to begin. Abhishek, knowing this was no ordinary debrief, took a breath and started outlining the situation.

"Ihfaaz was shot last night," Abhishek began. "He's recovering and claims he has no idea who could be behind the attack. But, with his connections, it's difficult to take that at face value."

Arun and Vikram listened intently, their faces neutral but eyes sharp. Abhishek continued, recounting the car explosion. "This morning, we found a burnt-out car on the outskirts of Sultanabad. At first, we thought it was an isolated incident, but after reviewing CCTV footage, we confirmed it was the same car used by the assassins in last night's shooting."

Arun's grip on his coffee cup tightened subtly, though his face remained expressionless. Vikram, too, leaned in slightly as the significance of the car explosion became clear.

"It's obvious," Abhishek said, "whoever orchestrated the hit wanted no loose ends. They made sure the assassins were silenced. Their bodies were burnt beyond recognition, which makes identification difficult. I've already submitted their fingerprints to the central crime database, but the process is taking longer than expected. If you could assist in expediting that, Mr. Arun Singh, it would be of great help."

Arun nodded but didn't comment, indicating he would make the necessary arrangements.

Abhishek picked up his iPad and opened a folder containing images from both crime scenes. As he handed the device to Vikram and Arun, he walked them through the details.

"We found empty bullet shells at both scenes—inside the car and at the site of the shooting. Upon analysis, we discovered the bullets recovered from Ihfaaz's body match the ones found at the car blast site. Additionally, we recovered firearms from the burnt vehicle. Preliminary ballistics confirmed they were the same weapons used in the attack."

Vikram zoomed in on the images of the burnt-out car, the blackened metal contorted from the blast, and the scattered bullet casings. He meticulously examined the pictures, noting every detail—the guns, the charred remains, and the positioning of the bodies. Arun looked over his shoulder, his face still unreadable.

"There's another element that complicates the investigation," Abhishek added. "We recovered partially burnt ID cards from the car. There were three bodies, and the IDs seem to belong to three different men. However, the details are badly damaged—names and addresses mostly burnt away. What we can make out suggests these men came from Kushalgram, a remote district near the border."

The mention of Kushalgram drew a faint flicker of surprise from Arun Singh. It was brief, but Abhishek noticed. Vikram, still holding the iPad, paused for a moment before zooming in on the half-burnt IDs. He remained silent, but the tension in the room shifted subtly.

"This is where it gets more puzzling," Abhishek continued, his voice steady. "Kushalgram is a long way from Sultanabad. Why would men from such a distant place, equipped with advanced weaponry, come all the way here to carry out this hit? It doesn't add up."

Vikram handed the iPad back to Abhishek, his expression thoughtful but composed. Arun, still leaning back in his chair, set down his coffee cup. His face, though calm, had grown more serious.

"Abhishek," Arun spoke now with more familiarity, having dispensed with the formal 'ji.' "If it's alright, I'd prefer to just call you by your name."

Abhishek nodded. "Of course, sir."

Arun leaned forward slightly. "You've done a thorough job so far. We'll expedite the fingerprint results. I'll make sure of that. But for now, focus on what you can uncover locally. We'll handle the larger aspects of this operation from our end. Keep your investigation tight and under wraps. No leaks."

Abhishek nodded, though he felt a growing sense of unease. The deeper he got into this case, the clearer it became that Ihfaaz wasn't just some high-profile hawala operator. His reach extended far beyond what Abhishek had initially thought.

After Abhishek left the Government Guest House, Arun Singh excused himself and retreated to his room. The quietude of the room contrasted sharply with the urgency of his task. He dialled a number and issued specific instructions to one of his officers stationed at Kushalgram.

Returning to the main room, Arun found Vikram waiting. "Please call Abhishek and ask him when they can arrange a meeting with Ihfaaz tomorrow," Arun said.

Vikram nodded and made the call. When he reached Abhishek, the conversation was brief. Abhishek agreed to check with the hospital and get back to Vikram with a suitable time for the meeting.

Meanwhile, Nadia had returned to the hospital to check on Ihfaaz. The sight of him, though markedly improved from the previous day, was still one of concern. His condition required vigilant medical supervision, and he was clearly exhausted. Nadia approached his bedside, relief etched on her face as she inquired about his health and the daily business operations.

They chatted briefly about the day's routine and the state of the business, which seemed to reassure Ihfaaz. "I'm glad to hear business is running smoothly and that there have been no panic withdrawals," Ihfaaz said.

However, the doctor on duty soon approached and requested that Nadia leave so that Ihfaaz could rest.

Before Nadia left, she mentioned that she had been receiving missed calls from a number listed as "A" but had refrained from calling back without consulting him first.

"Should I return the call?" Nadia asked.

The doctor had previously advised Ihfaaz to avoid using his phone for the time being. Despite this, Ihfaaz insisted Nadia dial the number and hand the phone to him. Nadia complied, watching curiously as Ihfaaz spoke briefly with the caller. The conversation was terse and uninformative; he assured the caller that he was traveling and would be unavailable for the next two to three days.

Nadia's curiosity was piqued. She had noticed that Ihfaaz hadn't disclosed the identity of the caller or the nature of their relationship. After the call ended, she asked, "Was that someone I know?"

Ihfaaz's gaze was steady, but there was an enigmatic quality to his response. "You will know when the time is right."

Nadia, puzzled yet resolute, left the hospital and headed straight to the office. The unanswered questions and the secretive phone call had only deepened her resolve. She had decided that once Ihfaaz was better, he would have to provide answers—especially regarding the identity of the mysterious caller and the deeper connections that seemed to be emerging.

The next morning, Arun Singh, Vikram, and Abhishek gathered at the Government Guest House before heading to the hospital to visit Ihfaaz. Upon entering the ICU, they found Ihfaaz propped up by a couple of pillows. His complexion was pale, his face still marked by the fatigue of recovery, but his eyes were sharp, showing that his mind was alert despite his weakened body. His breathing was measured, each movement calculated to avoid aggravating his injuries, though it was evident that his condition had improved since the shooting.

Arun Singh motioned to Abhishek, Vikram, and the on-duty doctor and nurses to wait outside, ensuring privacy for the conversation that was about to take place. Once they were alone, Arun Singh turned to Ihfaaz, the usually stoic man now softened with a look of concern. His expression resembled that of a caring elder, though the weight of what he was about to discuss loomed over the moment.

"So, what's the latest?" asked Ihfaaz, his voice raspy but steady.

Arun Singh approached the bedside and sat down, his face still carrying the mask of concern. He began by updating Ihfaaz on the details of the car blast and the ongoing investigation. Though the local police were still trying to piece together the identity of the attackers and the mastermind behind the hit, Arun Singh had already connected the dots.

"Thanks to the central crime database," Arun began, "I was able to confirm that the men who carried out the attack belonged to the vicinity of Kushalgram. Their names were Rizwan Sheikh, Faheem Ali, and Shabir Khan. They were the same men who had been contracted to kill you after the incident with Varda and followed you all the way to Kolkata. All evidence points to Fazil Hussain."

At the mention of Fazil Hussain, a shadow passed over Ihfaaz's face. His body tensed as if reacting to the name itself. Arun Singh noticed and immediately regretted bringing up the name at such a delicate time, but it was too late to retract his words. He continued, his voice softer, more cautious now.

"Somehow, Fazil must have found out that Ahsan is still alive. That name still burns in his mind. When he learned you survived, he sent those men to finish the job. Even after all these years, he still harbours that hatred towards you. While there's no direct proof of his involvement, all the signs point to him. He's ventured into more illegal activities, most likely with Varda's husband—his son-in-law. They're making more money than ever before, and that kind of power can feed a lot of grudges."

Hearing this, Ihfaaz's face shifted, his expression darkening. Arun Singh feared he had committed a blunder by revealing such sensitive information. Yet, after a long pause, Ihfaaz softly said, "Thank you for taking the trouble, sir."

Arun Singh, relieved but still cautious, leaned forward. "Now that your identity has been leaked, you need to be careful. I know you're thinking about revenge, but don't act impulsively. Let me handle Fazil Hussain. You've been through enough, and this is not the time for you to get involved."

"No," Ihfaaz replied firmly. "I'll deal with it once I'm out of this hospital."

Arun Singh immediately countered; his tone stricter. "No, Ihfaaz. I will handle this. You just focus on your recovery. Trust me, when we're done with that bastard Fazil, you'll be more than satisfied. I guarantee you'll see that no revenge of your own would match what we have planned. Let us take care of him."

Ihfaaz fell silent, his gaze drifting toward the window. He knew Arun Singh well enough to trust him, but something in him resisted the idea of letting others handle his personal vendetta. Arun Singh, sensing his hesitation, changed the subject.

"There's one more thing," Arun Singh said, his voice softening again. "I think it's time to let bygones be bygones. Let me contact my old friend Faraz and let him know that his youngest son is alive. He deserves to know."

Ihfaaz didn't respond, his face impassive. Arun Singh pressed on, his tone almost pleading. "Please, Ahsan. I consider you my own son. I'm asking you as a favour to me. I'm retiring in four months, and this would be my last request. You've done so much for us, for N.E.ST. You never once asked for anything in return. Let us show our gratitude by helping you now."

A tear welled up in Ihfaaz's eye, the weight of years in hiding, of severed family ties, catching up with him. He nodded, though his voice trembled slightly when he spoke. "You can inform my father, but if it ever comes to a point where my family insists on coming here, only my mother will be allowed. No one else."

Arun Singh groaned, frustrated but understanding. "Come on, Ahsan. Please reconsider."

"That condition is non-negotiable," Ihfaaz replied, his voice firm once more.

Arun Singh sighed in resignation. "Okay," he said finally, "if that's how you want it."

As he stood to leave, a small glimmer of hope crossed Arun Singh's mind. At least there had been a start—a fragile but significant step toward reuniting Ihfaaz with his past.

Chapter 33

In the late evening, Arun Singh, Vikram, and Abhishek gathered for another meeting. Arun Singh handed over a file to Abhishek, containing the results of the fingerprint scan from the Central Crime database. Abhishek flipped through the pages, astonished at the speed with which the results had been processed.

"Impressive," Abhishek remarked.

Arun Singh nodded. "We try to be efficient. I think we've also identified the person behind the attack."

Abhishek's eyebrows raised in anticipation. "You have a suspect?"

Arun Singh leaned back, his tone measured. "Yes. Though there's no concrete evidence directly linking him or his family to the crime, we have strong reasons to believe that he's responsible. Unfortunately, those reasons aren't something we can share with you right now."

Abhishek's expression shifted to one of confusion, sensing something unusual in the response. Arun Singh noticed the change and quickly added, "There are reasons that must remain classified. I understand this may be difficult for you to accept, but due to the lack of hard evidence, you won't be able to make any arrests."

Abhishek's sense of duty kicked in. "But sir, what about justice? Shouldn't we pursue your leads and try to gather more evidence? We might be able to nail the culprit if we push a little harder."

Arun Singh shook his head, his voice calm but resolute. "That won't be necessary. We will handle that part. It would be best if this case doesn't drag on. If needed, you can alter some of the details, perhaps change the official cause of the car explosion, and close the case quietly."

The idea of manipulating facts didn't sit well with Abhishek. He glanced at Vikram, who had remained silent for most of the meeting. For a fleeting second, a surprised expression crossed Vikram's face, but it quickly disappeared, replaced by his usual impassive expression.

Abhishek pressed further. "And what about Ihfaaz? He's bound to ask questions, especially with how closely involved I've become in this case. Won't he create issues when he learns we've closed the investigation without a clear outcome?"

Arun Singh smiled slightly, his voice steady. "No, he won't. That's my promise to you."

Abhishek hesitated for a moment, then asked, "If it's alright with you, sir, can I ask a personal question?"

"Of course," Arun Singh replied, his tone encouraging.

"Who are you?" Abhishek asked, his eyes narrowing in curiosity. "What do you people do to wield so much clout? And why are you so deeply involved in Ihfaaz's matters? What's in it for him?"

Arun Singh's smile widened slightly, as if he had been expecting the question. "Son, you're a sharp officer, one of the best I've seen. It wasn't easy to influence you—you take your duty very seriously, and I respect that. Some day, maybe, you'll find out who we are. Maybe you'll even work with us."

Abhishek listened carefully, knowing that Arun Singh wasn't giving much away but feeling that something important was left unsaid.

"When that day comes," Arun Singh continued, "you'll get all the answers you seek. You'll understand why we're doing this for Ihfaaz, and why we needed your cooperation. But for now, let's leave this mystery untouched."

Realizing that the conversation was nearing its end and that there was little more he could extract, Abhishek stood up, shook hands with both Arun Singh and Vikram, and excused himself.

Behind him, Arun Singh and Vikram remained, now alone, ready to attend to other pressing matters.

Vikram, feeling increasingly puzzled by the day's events, finally mustered the courage to ask Arun Singh what had been troubling him all morning. "Sir, what exactly is going on? First, you had a private meeting with Ihfaaz, without anyone present. And now you have the identity of the person behind the attack but aren't sharing it with the police. I can't make sense of it."

Arun Singh, sensing Vikram's confusion, nodded in understanding. "I knew you'd have questions. But before I explain, you need to listen to a story from my time at Kushalgram, when I was handling covert operations along the border."

He then launched into the tale of Ahsan, Faraz Khan, Fazil Hussain, and Varda—how Ahsan was betrayed by the girl he loved, Varda, how he was left isolated by his family, and how this abandonment drove him to death.

As Arun Singh finished, Vikram was in disbelief. "But what does a dead young man, his parents, and that girl and her family have to do with us now?" he asked, still trying to piece everything together.

Arun Singh leaned forward, his voice calm but serious. "That 'dead young man' is Ihfaaz. He loved Varda, but she used him and falsely accused him of something he never did. Betrayed by his family and the world, Ahsan—now Ihfaaz—channelled his anger and intelligence into a new life. At the age of 21 or 22, he faked his death, and I, with all my experience, didn't see it coming. He outfoxed us all and created a new empire from nothing in just 15 years."

Vikram, wide-eyed, interrupted. "He did all that at just 21? It's unbelievable."

Arun Singh nodded gravely. "Yes. He had a brilliant mind. He was supposed to pursue his master's, but the circumstances misdirected him. Over these years, he built a vast empire—partly legitimate, partly in the shadows—but now, his past has come back to haunt him. And that past concerns us, too. Ihfaaz has been a crucial asset to our operations."

Vikram looked at him, startled. "How exactly?"

"The information he provides, updates us on everything—from potential spies to honey trappers. Thanks to him, our success rate in intelligence has been significantly higher. The irony is that Ihfaaz himself doesn't fully realize the extent of how much he's helped us. We've kept it from him because we don't want him using that information to gain leverage over us. But in all these years, he's never once asked for a favour. That speaks volumes about his character."

Arun Singh paused, his expression turning solemn. "His father, Faraz Khan, was also a good friend of mine. During my time at Kushalgram, Faraz helped me in countless ways. Both father and son, even from within their illegal business operations, have done more for this country than most will ever know. And while they might never be recognized for it, their contributions have been invaluable."

Vikram's mind reeled as he tried to absorb the magnitude of what he was hearing. "But now Ihfaaz is focused on revenge, isn't he?" he asked.

Arun Singh sighed. "Yes, and that's the real problem. Once he's fully recovered, all his attention will be on settling the score with Fazil Hussain and his family. But we can't let that happen. Anger, especially when driven by revenge, only leads to destruction. A man filled with rage only harms himself in the end. It's like striking at the wind—he'll think he's hurting his enemy, but all he'll do is hurt himself. That's why I've convinced him to let us take care of Fazil Hussain for him."

Vikram nodded slowly, beginning to understand. "So, we're going to handle it?"

"Exactly," Arun Singh confirmed. "We need to think of ways to neutralize Fazil Hussain without letting Ihfaaz get consumed by his own anger. We'll work together to find a solution. Ihfaaz has been through enough, and the last thing we need is for him to destroy himself in his pursuit of vengeance."

Arun Singh then stood up and glanced at his watch. "Now, I need to call my old friend, Faraz Khan, and tell him that his youngest son is still alive. It's not going to be an easy conversation, but it's long overdue."

Vikram watched as Arun Singh left the room, still processing everything he had just learned.

Chapter 34

Faraz Khan was sitting in his office, absorbed in reviewing some documents, when his phone buzzed. It was an unknown number, and with a hint of curiosity, he answered the call. The voice on the other end was familiar yet unexpected—Arun Kumar Singh.

"Faraz bhai, Arun Singh here. How are you?" Arun Singh's tone was warm but carried a note of gravity.

Faraz Khan, caught off guard, was initially silent, trying to grasp the significance of the call. After exchanging some pleasantries and catching up briefly, Arun Singh moved to the crux of the conversation.

"Faraz bhai, I have some very good news to share with you," Arun Singh began.

Faraz's interest was piqued. "What is it?"

Arun Singh took a deep breath before delivering the news. "Ahsan is alive. He is currently in Sultanabad, Maharashtra."

The revelation struck Faraz like a thunderbolt. For a moment, he was speechless, his mind reeling with disbelief and a flood of emotions. He had been living with the pain of his son's loss for years, and now to hear that he was alive was almost too much to process.

Arun Singh, sensing the emotional impact of his words, continued with concern. "Faraz bhai, I understand this news is overwhelming. I need you to remain calm and composed. I have more details to share, but it's crucial that you do not disclose this information to anyone, not even your family, for now."

Faraz's voice trembled as he asked, "How? Where? What happened?"

Arun Singh replied, "It's a long story. I can explain everything in detail when we meet. For now, I need you to come to Sultanabad as soon as possible, along with your wife. Once you are here, I will explain everything to you in person. You can then disclose the news to your wife. Please understand, this situation is sensitive and involves the security of your son's life. I would not ask this of you if it weren't necessary."

Faraz Khan, overwhelmed and struggling to contain his emotions, managed to reply, "Alright, Arun bhai. I'll make arrangements to come with my wife. But please, tell me more about what's going on."

Arun Singh, maintaining his calm, said, "I will give you all the details once you arrive. For now, focus on getting here quickly. It's important for your safety and your son's. I'll be waiting for you."

The call ended, leaving Faraz Khan sitting in stunned silence, tears welling up in his eyes. He had to process the reality that his son, presumed dead for so long, was alive. As he prepared to inform his wife and make the necessary arrangements, the weight of the news and the urgency of the situation settled heavily on him.

As Ihfaaz was shifted from the ICU to a private room, the atmosphere in his part of the hospital wing was calm and quiet. The room was sparsely decorated, and the only occupants were Ihfaaz and his two visitors: Nadia and Pradip. The change in Ihfaaz's condition was notable; he was far better than he had been three days ago, though still visibly weak.

Nadia entered the room first, followed shortly by Pradip. They greeted Ihfaaz with warm smiles, and Pradip updated him on the latest news.

"Dinu Kaka is really eager to see you, but his health is preventing him from coming down. His son, Samir, will come over whenever you say it's okay," Pradip informed Ihfaaz. "There's been an outpouring of support—phone calls, messages, personal visits from everyone who cares about you. It's clear you have a lot of people who want to see you recover quickly."

Ihfaaz was moved by the show of support. "It's overwhelming," he said, his voice soft with gratitude. "But let's talk about something else. How is everything going with the business?"

Nadia, clearly concerned for Ihfaaz's health, interjected firmly. "You need to focus on getting better, not worrying about business matters."

There was a moment of silence in the room as they all absorbed the gravity of the situation. Then Ihfaaz, mustering his courage, decided to share something important. "I need to tell you both something," he began, looking at Nadia and Pradip. "You are the closest I have to family these days. So, you deserve to know this first. I have a past that neither of you knows about. In fact, no one from my current life knows about it. This incident has intertwined my past and present in ways I didn't expect."

He turned his gaze to Nadia with a hint of mischief. "The mysterious caller you wanted to know about? She is my mother. My parents, or at least my mother might be arriving soon. Please make arrangements for their stay here. And don't disclose in front of anybody that you know that I am in touch with my mother. As for the rest of the story, I promise I'll disclose more soon."

Nadia, stunned by the sudden revelation, was at a loss for words. She had been trying to uncover the mystery of Ihfaaz's past for so long, and now, just when she was least expecting it, he was finally opening up. "Of course, Ihfaaz. I'll take care of the arrangements. Is there anything else you need?"

Ihfaaz's eyes lit up with a hint of nostalgia. "I'd love to have a cigarette, though I don't know if the doctors will permit it."

Nadia, maintaining her firm stance, shook her head. "No way, not now nor ever. Anything else?"

Ihfaaz chuckled, "Alright, just a plate of nice chicken fried rice. I'm tired of this hospital food."

Nadia smiled and agreed, then left the room to get the food.

With Nadia gone, Pradip turned to Ihfaaz and smiled. "What are you smiling about?" Ihfaaz asked, noticing the expression on Pradip's face.

Pradip replied, "When are you going to accept it? It's clear that Nadia is madly in love with you, and it seems like you have feelings for her too."

Ihfaaz shook his head. "No, there's nothing like that."

Pradip's expression softened. "Nadia is like my younger sister. She never hides anything from me. She's a great person who genuinely cares about you. You need to think about settling down now. This is your chance."

Ihfaaz sighed, "Pradip bhai, my life is complicated. I don't want to bring anyone else into this mess."

Pradip's tone was firm but caring. "Those are just excuses. I strongly recommend you settle down with Nadia as soon as you can. The rest is up to you."

Chapter 35

The sun had just risen and chaos erupted in Fazil Hussain's life. Multiple departments—police, excise, narcotics, income tax, GST, and food and drugs—simultaneously raided his home, office, and even the residence of his daughter. The operation was swift and thorough, leaving no corner untouched.

Fazil Hussain, along with his sons and son-in-law, found themselves arrested under various charges. Bank accounts were frozen, offices and vehicles were sealed, and all the gold and cash in the house was confiscated. Fazil Hussain's once-thriving empire had come crashing down in what seemed like a matter of hours.

Confused and desperate, Fazil Hussain tried reaching out to his numerous contacts within these departments, but none of them answered his calls. He had suddenly become an outcast, and his family was left to fend for themselves amidst the chaos.

In the police lock-up, Fazil Hussain, his son and his son in law were confronted with a single demand: confess to sending three contract killers to Sultanabad. Despite their denials and claims of ignorance, the authorities pressed on. They maintained their innocence, claiming no knowledge of Sultanabad or the alleged conspiracy.

After a gruelling week in captivity, they were finally allowed to meet their family. The ordeal had visibly aged Fazil Hussain, who looked decades older. His sons and son-in-law were battered and exhausted, having been deprived of sleep and subjected to harsh conditions. The women in the family, overwhelmed and anxious, tried to console one another but felt powerless in the face of their grim situation. Their lawyers struggled to navigate the overwhelming number of cases against them. Even if they managed to secure bail in one case, another department would take custody and re-arrest them, keeping them ensnared in a relentless cycle.

As they left the police station, a police constable approached Varda, Fazil Hussain's daughter. The constable, an older man who appeared to be around Fazil Hussain's age, quietly informed her of a potential lead. "You need to get in touch with one Ihfaaz Khan in Sultanabad," he said. "From what I've gathered, everything started with an attack on Ihfaaz Khan, who is quite influential. Evidence is pointing towards your family, and if Ihfaaz Khan could help you, it might resolve this issue."

Varda, stunned but hopeful, thanked the constable and left the police station with a sense of urgency. She understood that contacting Ihfaaz Khan might be their only chance to turn things around.

Meanwhile, the police station in-charge had been observing the conversation from a window on the first floor. As the constable returned to his boss's cabin, the in-charge asked him, "Did you tell her what you were supposed to?"

"Yes, sir," the constable replied.

The in-charge then asked, "What are the chances of her going to Sultanabad?"

The constable responded, "She's very desperate. I believe she will go."

"Alright," the in-charge said, "If she doesn't go, I'll ensure she has no other choice. She will need to visit Ihfaaz Khan, come what may."

The in-charge's mind was set on ensuring Varda's visit to Sultanabad, motivated by his own desire to avoid the wrath of his superiors. He had no interest in the underlying motives or the broader implications of the situation. His only goal was to see the task completed and return to his normal routine, away from the relentless pressure of his superiors.

Chapter 36

The next morning, Arun Singh, accompanied by Vikram, visited Ihfaaz at the hospital. They were pleased to see him looking better, sitting in a chair, enjoying his breakfast. Ihfaaz welcomed them warmly and offered tea or coffee, though they politely declined, having already eaten.

After some casual conversation, Arun Singh got straight to the main topic: the raids conducted on Fazil Hussain's properties the previous day. He informed Ihfaaz that based on initial reports, it seemed like it would take months for Fazil Hussain to secure bail. Ihfaaz, mildly surprised by the news, listened carefully. Arun Singh added that within 8 to 10 days, Varda would likely come to Sultanabad, which seemed to catch Ihfaaz off guard.

Arun Singh reassured him, explaining that the strategy was meticulous. "The way we have operated," he said, "I doubt Fazil Hussain will even have enough money for basic medications, let alone try anything against you again. As for Varda, she needs to face the consequences of her past actions. That's why we ensured she would be compelled to come here."

Arun Singh then shifted the conversation to a more personal matter. "Your parents will arrive in Sultanabad by late evening," he told Ihfaaz, who was about to comment on his father. Before he could speak, Arun interrupted, "Look, Ihfaaz, your father will only come to meet you if you give the go-ahead. As of now, only he knows the full truth about his youngest son. Your mother will be told when they arrive in Sultanabad. Apart from Faraz Khan, no one else knows that Ahsan is still alive."

Arun Singh expressed that arrangements would be needed for their stay, but Ihfaaz quickly assured him that he had already taken care of it. He added that Nadia would coordinate with Vikram regarding the specifics of their accommodation. Arun nodded, feeling relieved that Ihfaaz was still as sharp and organized as ever, despite his condition.

Before leaving, Arun mentioned that he would be departing Sultanabad later that night after briefing Ihfaaz's father. Vikram, however, would stay for a few more days to assist. As Arun reached the door, Nadia walked in. Ihfaaz introduced Arun Singh and Vikram but refrained from revealing their true identities or his connection to them. He then instructed Nadia to coordinate with Vikram on his parents' arrangements, to which she agreed, though she seemed curious about the conversation.

Just as Arun Singh was about to leave, Ihfaaz called out to him. "Sir, thank you," he said with a deep sense of gratitude. Arun smiled and nodded before exiting the room with Vikram, leaving Ihfaaz and Nadia alone.

The anticipation that had been building all day for Ihfaaz felt almost unbearable. His mother, whom he hadn't seen in over 15 years, was finally arriving, though his feelings towards his father were more complicated. The evening brought with it the arrival of his parents in Sultanabad. Arun Singh and Vikram personally received them and took them to the hotel Nadia had booked. Following Ihfaaz's instructions, Nadia greeted them professionally without introducing herself, and after settling them in their room, she and Vikram excused themselves, saying they would be waiting downstairs.

Once alone with them, Arun Singh carefully disclosed the truth behind their visit. Shahana, Ihfaaz's mother, was immediately overwhelmed by the revelation that her son, whom she thought was dead, had been alive all these years. She burst into uncontrollable sobs, holding onto her husband, who silently comforted her. Faraz Khan, already emotionally drained from earlier conversations with Arun, maintained his composure but couldn't hide the sorrow and regret etched on his face.

Arun went on to tell them about the attack on Ihfaaz and reassured them that their son was recovering well. This news struck Shahana like a blow. She cried even harder, the thought of her son suffering once again too much for her to bear. After several minutes of sobbing, she finally gathered herself and made one simple request: "Please, I want to see my son. Take me to him."

Arun, with a gentle smile, replied, "That's why Nadia and Vikram are waiting downstairs. They will take you to him." Together, they made their way to the hospital.

Upon reaching the third floor, where Ihfaaz's room was located, Arun Singh stopped Faraz Khan at the hallway, pressing his shoulder gently. "Bhai, I think it's better you and I wait here. Ahsan still harbours anger towards you. He said he needs more time before he can meet you."

Faraz's face drained of colour as the weight of Arun's words hit him. His eyes filled with tears. "Arun bhai," he whispered, his voice breaking, "What have I done to deserve this? Haven't I been punished enough? For 15 years, I have cried, repented for how I treated him, and now that I know he's alive, my son won't see me."

Arun Singh, feeling the depth of his friend's sorrow, placed a comforting hand on his shoulder. "Faraz bhai, I understand your pain. But give him some time. We've come this far. Maybe in a day or two, Ahsan will turn around. Let him have this moment with his mother for now."

With that, they both sat down in the waiting area, leaving Shahana to her long-overdue reunion with her son. Faraz Khan stared blankly ahead, a mix of hope and heartbreak swirling within him, praying for the moment his son might finally forgive him.

When Nadia and Shahana reached the door to Ihfaaz's room, she gently asked Vikram to wait outside. Taking a deep breath, Nadia opened the door and, with a warm smile, said, "Ihfaaz, look who has come to meet you!"

As soon as Ihfaaz turned his head and saw his mother standing there, his emotions overwhelmed him. Tears welled up in his eyes, and before he could stop himself, they began streaming down his face. "Ammi..." he managed to whisper before breaking into sobs. Shahana, seeing her son after 15 long years, couldn't hold back either. She rushed forward, her own tears falling uncontrollably, and took him into her arms, holding him close as if never wanting to let go.

Both mother and son sat there, crying like lost children finally reunited. Shahana caressed his head, her fingers running through his hair, while Ihfaaz, feeling the warmth and comfort of his mother after so many years of separation, sobbed like a little boy. The deep sorrow, guilt, and regret that had haunted both of them seemed to pour out in that moment, their tears speaking more than any words ever could.

Nadia stood by the door, watching this deeply emotional reunion. It was a moment of pure love and release, but as she watched them, a familiar ache settled in her heart. Silent tears began to fall from her own eyes as memories of her own mother surfaced. She hadn't realized how much she missed that motherly presence in her life until now. Nadia wiped her tears, trying to remain composed, but the reunion was too poignant to ignore.

After what felt like an eternity, with both mother and son still crying, Nadia gently approached them. She walked to the bed, holding a glass of water in her hand, and tenderly placed her hand on Shahana's shoulder. "Aunty," she said softly, her voice filled with care, "please stop crying. Calm down and take a sip of water. Look, you're making Ihfaaz cry too, and it's not good for him to cry like this. Please..."

Her tone was gentle, almost like a daughter comforting her own mother, full of affection and understanding. There was something about the way Nadia spoke that made it seem as though she was family, someone who truly cared for both of them. Shahana, still weeping, took the glass from Nadia with trembling hands and took a small sip, trying to calm herself. Then she turned to Ihfaaz, and with the same love that had always been her strength, said, "Ahsan, here, have a sip."

Ihfaaz, his eyes still brimming with tears, took the glass from her. He took a small sip of the water and managed to say, "Ammi..." before he began crying again. His voice cracked with emotion, as if all the years of separation and pain had been released in those simple words.

Eventually, after several more moments of shared tears, both mother and son managed to calm down. Shahana, wiping her eyes, finally smiled through her tears. She began fussing over Ihfaaz, her fingers gently tracing the lines of his face, as though memorizing every feature once again. "You've changed so much, my son," she said, her voice thick with emotion. "Your hair... your face..." She kissed his forehead lovingly, caressing his cheek with the tenderness only a mother could offer. "You've grown up so much, Ahsan."

Just as the atmosphere began to settle, Nadia, ever practical, brought in a tray filled with cakes and sweets. With a cheerful tone, she announced, “Now, enough of all this crying. This is a time for joy, not tears! We should eat something sweet to celebrate this reunion.” She offered a sweet to Shahana, who smiled gratefully and took it. Then she turned to Ihfaaz, who initially declined.

“No, I don’t want any,” Ihfaaz said, shaking his head slightly.

But Nadia wasn’t having it. “Oh, come on! You have to eat something. We can’t celebrate without you!” she insisted with a playful smile, her determination evident.

Finally, Ihfaaz gave in and took the piece of sweet. Before he could eat it, Shahana, like any mother would, made sure he took a bite first, watching him with love in her eyes. After he took a small bite, Shahana followed suit, taking a bite of her own.

Nadia, always quick with her humour, mock-pouted, “What about me? No one offered me anything!” She looked at them playfully, her eyes twinkling.

Shahana, smiling now, took another sweet and offered it to Nadia. “Here, my dear,” she said warmly, handing it to her. “And may you always be happy. You’ve brought so much joy to us today.”

Nadia, touched by Shahana’s gesture, accepted the sweet with a smile. As she took a bite, Shahana placed a hand on her head, blessing her. “May you be blessed with happiness and everything your heart desires.

As Nadia sat in the darkest corner of the hospital corridor, she let her tears flow freely, her heart aching with the longing for her own mother. Learning that Ihfaaz’s original name was Ahsan had stirred something deep within her, reminding her how little she knew about the man she had grown so fond of. The revelation added layers of mystery, and with it, a sense of distance. There was still so much to learn about his past, about the pain and the secrets he carried.

Meanwhile, in the room, Ihfaaz—Ahsan—and his mother, Shahana, were slowly reconnecting after years of separation. They had so much to catch up on, memories to share, and unspoken emotions to release. After a while, Shahana brought up a topic that had been heavy on her heart. "Ahsan," she began softly, "will you let your father meet you? Please, for my sake."

Ihfaaz's expression immediately hardened. "No, Ammi. He's the one who said he didn't want to talk to me anymore. Why take the trouble now?"

Shahana sighed deeply, her voice filled with quiet sorrow. "He has repented a lot in the last 15 years. He is still your father, no matter what happened."

Ihfaaz looked at his mother, the pain in his eyes still raw. After a long pause, he relented. "Okay, Ammi. Just because you're asking... but we'll meet tomorrow. I'm feeling too tired now. I need to sleep. Please understand."

A faint smile touched Shahana's lips as she nodded. "Alright, my love. Tomorrow, then."

As she stood to leave, she hesitated at the door and turned back with a playful glint in her eye. "Ahsan... do I have a daughter-in-law or grandchildren waiting to meet me?"

Ihfaaz laughed lightly for the first time in what felt like forever. "No, Ammi, I'm still unmarried."

"Hmmm..." Shahana replied with a knowing smile, then asked, "And who is this Nadia?"

"She works with me, Ammi," Ihfaaz said simply.

Shahana raised an eyebrow, her motherly intuition sparking. "Seems like she has a liking for you."

Ihfaaz rolled his eyes, half-smiling. "Ammi, I need to sleep. Goodnight."

"Goodnight, my son." Shahana kissed his forehead lovingly and left the room, making her way back to her husband. She thanked Arun Singh once again for reuniting her with her son and then told Faraz that Ahsan would meet him tomorrow. Faraz, visibly relieved, thanked God, his emotions too intense for words.

A short while later, Shahana called out to Nadia, who had been waiting quietly. "Beti, can you please escort us back to the hotel?"

Nadia, composed again, smiled warmly. "Aunty, I was waiting for you. Let's go."

Shahana noticed the dried tear streaks on Nadia's face but didn't comment. She sensed that this young woman, so full of kindness, had her own burdens to bear. During the car ride back to the hotel, and even throughout dinner, Shahana subtly inquired about Nadia's life. She asked about her family, how long she had known Ahsan, and other casual questions, but each one was calculated. Nadia, unaware of the subtle evaluation, answered openly, her heart clean and her words honest. Her sincerity only endeared her further to Shahana.

During dinner, Nadia couldn't help but fuss over how little Shahana and Faraz were eating, insisting they take more, making sure their plates were full. She smiled and served them with such genuine care that even Arun Singh, who was deep in conversation with Faraz, took notice. Nadia's warmth and attention didn't go unnoticed by Shahana either.

After dinner, Nadia escorted Shahana and Faraz to their room, ensuring they were comfortable and had everything they needed. As she prepared to leave, she smiled and promised, "I'll come back in the morning, and we'll have breakfast together before heading to the hospital to meet Ihfaaz."

Shahana, touched by Nadia's kindness, moved forward and kissed her forehead. "Beti, it's okay to miss your loved ones now and then, but until I'm here, consider me your mother."

Nadia's eyes filled with gratitude, and she hugged Shahana tightly. "Can I also call you Ammi?" she asked, her voice soft and hopeful.

Shahana smiled warmly. "Of course, my dear. That's what all my children call me."

Nadia left the hotel feeling a deep sense of happiness, her heart lighter than it had been in a long time. For the first time in years, she felt like she had found a place where she truly belonged.

Meanwhile, back in their room, Faraz and Shahana spent the night talking about Ahsan, about the years they had missed, and the emotions they had kept buried for so long. It seemed as if the night itself wasn't long enough to contain all the stories and feelings they had to share. The reunion had opened doors they thought were closed forever, and there was so much healing still left to do.

The morning of the much-anticipated reunion between Faraz Khan and his son, Ahsan, unfolded with a mix of anticipation and quiet tension. As Faraz, Shahana, and Nadia entered the hospital room, the atmosphere was heavy with expectation. Faraz had braced himself for an emotional outburst, but the reality was more subdued.

Ahsan sat by the balcony, his back to the room. When Faraz called out to him, Ahsan turned around. The sight was striking—Ahsan had transformed from the carefree youth he had once been into a mature man whose face was mostly impassive, save for his eyes. His eyes, however, told a different story. They were filled with a deep, emotive sadness, as if all the pain and suffering of the past 15 years had been contained within them, waiting to be released.

Faraz walked slowly toward his son, his heart heavy with a mix of hope and apprehension. As he spread his arms, Ahsan hesitated only for a moment before stepping forward to embrace his father. The embrace was both tender and poignant. Father and son clung to each other, tears flowing silently, their sobs a quiet testament to the years of lost time and unresolved pain. For five to ten minutes, they were lost in this embrace, the room echoing with their unspoken sorrow.

When Faraz finally broke the embrace, he kissed Ahsan's forehead and whispered, "I am sorry, Beta. I am sorry. I know I have wronged you in many ways. Please forgive me. Please forgive me." His voice broke once again, and he dissolved into tears.

Ahsan, holding his father, comforted him softly. "It's okay, Baba, it's okay. It's all over." His voice was calm, but there was a profound sadness in his words. Both father and son then took their seats on the bed, with Nadia and Shahana settling on the opposite couch. Nadia offered them water, her eyes reflecting her own emotional turmoil.

As the initial flood of emotions began to ebb, Faraz expressed his concern for Ahsan's well-being and his anger towards Fazil Hussain for once again endangering his son's life. Shahana, echoing Faraz's sentiments, added with bitterness, "May that Fazil Hussain and his daughter rot in hell."

Ahsan's response was quiet but resolute. "Very soon, Ammi, very soon."

The conversation then shifted to Ahsan's journey from Kolkata to Sultanabad. Ahsan briefly recounted the events, his voice steady despite the weight of the narrative. Faraz was both surprised and worried to learn about Ahsan's involvement in the hawala business, but he chose to keep his concerns to himself for the moment, prioritizing the peace they had achieved.

Faraz Khan then inquired about Arun Singh. "How did you meet Arun Singh? What role has he played in all this?"

Ahsan explained that he and Arun Singh shared common interests, and their paths had crossed due to mutual goals and objectives.

Just then, Pradip entered the room. Ahsan introduced him to his parents. The meeting was cordial, with Pradip exchanging polite greetings with Faraz and Shahana.

As the conversation continued, Shahana turned to Ahsan with a hesitant request. "Beta, would it be alright if we convey the news of your being alive to your brothers and sisters? And will you come back with us to Kushalgram?"

Ahsan fell silent, weighing his response. "Ammi, just give me some more time. You can convey the news to them when I am ready. As for coming to Kushalgram, I will visit for sure, but only for a few days. My home will always be here in Sultanabad. Please try to understand."

Shahana's eyes glistened with unshed tears, but she nodded understandingly. "We understand, Beta. We do understand."

Chapter 37

The following days were filled with a sense of warmth and harmony that Ihfaaz had not experienced in years. Having reunited with his parents, there was a noticeable change in him. He seemed more at peace, more jovial, and even a bit lighter in spirit. His parents, especially Shahana, noticed how his eyes sparkled differently now—especially when Nadia was around. She was a constant presence, always attending to his needs and ensuring his parents were comfortable.

Shahana couldn't help but notice the quiet affection that Nadia had for her son. It was in the way she looked at him, the way her face lit up when he called her name. But what surprised Shahana even more was the way Ihfaaz responded, though more subtly. He never voiced it, but his actions spoke volumes. If Nadia stepped out for more than a few minutes, he would call her back, his voice betraying an impatience he tried to hide.

One afternoon, as the three of them sat together—Shahana, Ihfaaz, and Nadia—the mood was light. They were laughing and talking when Nadia, out of curiosity, asked, "Ammi, who is Varda?"

The question, innocent as it seemed, changed the entire atmosphere. Ihfaaz's face tensed immediately, and he looked away, the pain in his expression unmistakable. Shahana, who had been smiling, grew silent. Nadia quickly realized her mistake and apologized, feeling she had crossed a boundary.

But Shahana, after a pause, spoke softly, "Ahsan, beta, she deserves to know. Look at how much she has done for you. Can't you see? She loves you, and you're being foolish not to acknowledge her feelings. Not every woman is like Varda, beta. Nadia is different, and she deserves the truth from you."

Ihfaaz remained quiet, his jaw clenched. He seemed reluctant, almost as if reopening old wounds would break him. But after a few moments of tense silence, he began speaking, his voice low and controlled.

"Varda..." he said, as if the name itself caused him pain. "Varda was the love of my life. I was madly in love with her."

He went on to narrate the story, speaking of how he had once loved Varda with every fibre of his being, how he had trusted her completely, only to have his heart shattered by her betrayal. He spoke of how he had ended up in Mumbai, lost and broken, and how the events following that betrayal had altered the course of his life forever. His voice was steady, but his words were filled with a deep, lingering sorrow.

When he finished, there was a long, painful silence. Then, suddenly, as if a dam inside him had burst, Ihfaaz took a deep breath and began to cry. His body shook with sobs as he cried out, "Why, Ammi? Why did she do this to me? Why did fate do this to me? Why did everyone do this to me? What was my fault, Ammi? What was my fault?"

Shahana, heartbroken at seeing her son in such anguish, embraced him tightly. "Beta," she whispered, her voice filled with maternal love and sorrow, "sometimes life tests us in ways we don't understand. But you have to remember, not everyone will hurt you like she did. Life can be cruel, but it can also give you second chances. Look at how far you've come, Ahsan. Look at the people who love you."

Still crying, Ihfaaz nestled into his mother's arms, his body shaking with grief as he relived the trauma of his past. Shahana gently caressed his hair, whispering words of comfort. Slowly, the intensity of his sobs lessened, and eventually, he drifted into sleep, exhausted from the emotional toll of the conversation.

Shahana held him close, her heart aching for her son's pain. Across the room, Nadia sat in stunned silence, her own face streaked with tears. The depth of Ihfaaz's suffering shook her, and in that moment, she silently vowed that she would do everything in her power to ensure that he would never suffer like this again. She would stand by him, protect him, and love him in a way that no one ever had.

After that conversation about Varda, the name was never brought up again. It seemed to drift into the past, allowing Ihfaaz and Nadia to grow closer, and for Nadia's bond with his parents to strengthen. Shahana often referred to Nadia as her daughter, and the warmth between them was undeniable. Even Faraz, a man of few words, had taken a liking to her, appreciating how she had become an integral part of his son's life.

During their time together, Faraz silently observed the events unfolding around Ihfaaz. He came to know about the raids and subsequent arrest of Fazil Hussain and his sons. Though they never discussed it openly, he was aware that his son had orchestrated the raids and the arrest of Fazil Hussain and his sons. From the quiet conversations, the subtle glances exchanged between Ihfaaz and his contacts, and the sense of control he seemed to have over the situation, it was clear to Faraz. He didn't bring it up, perhaps out of fear of opening old wounds.

Ten days after getting shot, the time finally came for Ihfaaz to be discharged from the hospital. His recovery had been swift, thanks to his resilience, but also to the unrelenting care of his mother and Nadia. A couple of days after the discharge, it was time for Faraz and Shahana to leave. The room was filled with mixed emotions. Shahana clung to him a little longer than usual, her hands lingering on his shoulders, her eyes full of tears. Faraz, though more reserved, placed his hand on his son's back as a quiet gesture of support.

"Stay in touch, beta," Shahana had whispered tearfully.

"I will, Ammi. Just wait a bit longer before telling the others about me. Please," Ihfaaz had requested.

They had respected his wishes, though the longing to reunite the entire family was evident. Teary-eyed, Shahana and Faraz left

Sultanabad, leaving behind their son, but with hope in their hearts for the future.

As the days passed, Ihfaaz resumed his work, much to Nadia's annoyance. She worried that he was pushing himself too soon after the trauma, both physical and emotional. Despite her protests, he was determined to immerse himself in the office and the world he had built in Sultanabad. Nadia found herself constantly trying to make sure he wasn't overexerting himself, bringing him food, reminding him to rest, yet all of it seemed to fall on deaf ears.

Her frustration grew further because of Abhishek. During Ihfaaz's stay in the hospital, Abhishek had visited him three or four times, and on two occasions had insisted on speaking to Ihfaaz alone. Nadia felt a surge of distrust whenever he appeared. From the moment they met, there had been tension between them. Abhishek's cold behaviour, his clinical approach, and the way he had spoken to her on that first day had left a sour taste in her mouth.

One afternoon, as they sat in the office, she finally brought it up to Ihfaaz. "You know, I really don't like how Abhishek behaved with me," she said, frustration evident in her voice. "The way he treated me that first day at the hospital, like I was just someone to be interrogated... it was humiliating."

Ihfaaz, ever the calm mediator, leaned back in his chair and looked at her thoughtfully. "Nadia, Abhishek was just doing his job. In situations like mine, everyone is a suspect at first. He had to investigate thoroughly."

"That doesn't justify his rudeness," Nadia retorted, folding her arms.

"I understand how you feel," Ihfaaz said softly, "but you have to admit, he did a great job with the investigation. It wasn't personal."

Nadia bit her lip, feeling the sting of his words. She didn't like how Ihfaaz was defending Abhishek, and more than anything, she didn't like how it made her feel as though her concerns weren't valid. She stayed quiet, but inside, the discomfort lingered. She felt as though Ihfaaz was brushing aside her feelings, taking Abhishek's side instead of hers.

Abhishek's Story

Abhishek had always been a sincere student. From his school days, he had idolized his father, Inspector Giriraj Patil, who toiled day and night in the service of the Mumbai police force. It was his father's unflinching dedication to duty that sparked in him a desire to succeed, to live a life marked by purpose and integrity. When Abhishek secured admission into an engineering college in Pune, it felt like the first significant step toward making his father proud.

For the first few months, everything went smoothly. The college was competitive but rewarding, and Abhishek found a close-knit group of friends who shared his ambitions. One evening, as the group celebrated a friend's birthday in their hostel room, Abhishek's life took an unexpected turn.

Laughter echoed off the walls of the cramped room as bottles were passed around, the atmosphere carefree and wild. They had no idea that their celebration would be cut short in the most jarring manner possible. Without warning, the door was kicked open, and the hostel warden, flanked by stern-looking security guards, stormed in. The guards were unfamiliar—new faces who had clearly been brought in for this very purpose. One of them carrying a camera started snapping pictures of the chaos as the students froze in confusion and terror.

They were dragged out into the passage, made to stand in a line like criminals. As their room was ransacked, their belongings thrown about, the boys were forced to strip down and submit to searches. Every attempt to explain themselves was met with cold indifference. After two hours of humiliating treatment, the verdict was delivered: they had been caught consuming alcohol in the hostel, and immediate disciplinary action would follow.

At first, the boys joked about their fate. They assumed that at worst, they'd be rusticated for a week or two. It wasn't until the next morning that the gravity of the situation truly hit.

Abhishek returned home to Mumbai, but he couldn't bring himself to tell his father what had happened. It was only when Giriraj received a phone call from the college the next morning that the full weight of the disaster was revealed. The college had rusticated Abhishek, pending a formal inquiry by a disciplinary committee. Worse yet, if the committee found him guilty, not only would he be permanently expelled, but he would also be blacklisted by the university, and the case would be handed over to the police.

For the first time in his life, Abhishek saw his future slipping away.

His father was furious. Abhishek bore the brunt of his anger, receiving a severe thrashing. But what stung more than the physical pain was the disappointment in his father's eyes. A hearing was scheduled, and though Abhishek and Giriraj presented their side of the story, it became clear that the committee had already made up its mind. The decision would be rendered in a month, but that month felt like a lifetime. Every avenue they pursued seemed blocked, and Giriraj's frustration grew with each passing day.

Then, someone made a suggestion that could change everything. If Giriraj conducted a raid on Dinesh Patel's premises and secured his arrest, the disciplinary committee could be "managed." It was an unspoken agreement—one that Giriraj loathed but felt compelled to accept for the sake of his son's future.

The raid was carried out. But instead of Dinesh Patel, Ihfaaz was the one arrested. A twist of fate, a miscalculation. Giriraj tried every trick in the book to pressure Ihfaaz into incriminating Patel, but the man refused to cooperate. Giriraj's nerves were frayed under the weight of impending failure, while Abhishek sank deeper into helplessness, resigned to whatever punishment awaited him.

Then, something unexpected happened. Giriraj informed Abhishek that Ihfaaz wanted to meet him. Abhishek was shocked. Why would a man caught in the crossfire of his father's desperation want to help him? Nevertheless, the meeting took place.

Ihfaaz's demeanour was calm, composed. Over several discussions, he listened as Abhishek recounted the events leading up to the raid. He asked about the profiles of the committee members, the politics at play, and the undercurrents of the situation. To Abhishek's astonishment, Ihfaaz reassured him that everything would be taken care of. "Don't worry," he said. "You'll be back in college soon."

True to his word, when the disciplinary committee rendered its verdict: Abhishek was found not guilty. He was asked to resume his studies immediately. The sense of relief was overwhelming. Abhishek could scarcely believe his fortune. He returned to the hostel as if nothing had ever happened, but deep inside, he knew he owed his future to Ihfaaz.

Gratitude was an understatement for what he felt toward the man who had saved him. When Abhishek finished his engineering degree, he made a bold declaration: he wanted to work for Ihfaaz. His father, already uneasy about the murky dealings that surrounded Ihfaaz, was heartbroken. Giriraj had wanted so much more for his son—anything but a life in the underworld. But Abhishek was resolute.

It was Ihfaaz himself who eventually convinced Abhishek to take a different path. "You're meant for greater things," he told him, urging him to prepare for the competitive exams that would lead to a career in civil service. Ihfaaz used his considerable influence to get Abhishek enrolled in one of the best IAS/IPS coaching institutes. On his second attempt, Abhishek cleared the IPS exams.

The first person he called after sharing the news with his parents was Ihfaaz. "I've made it," he said, barely able to contain his excitement. Ihfaaz congratulated him warmly, offering his best wishes for a bright future.

Years passed, and Abhishek's career blossomed. Ihfaaz remained in the background, a guiding force whenever Abhishek sought his advice. Many times, Abhishek expressed his desire to repay the man who had done so much for him, but Ihfaaz always brushed it off, saying, "When the time is right, I'll ask for a favour."

That time came six months before the shooting incident. Ihfaaz had arranged for Abhishek to be transferred to Sultanabad. The moment Abhishek received his posting, he called Ihfaaz, thrilled to be closer to his mentor. But Ihfaaz's response was unexpected. "We must cease all communication from this point on," he said. "No one should know that we're connected."

Abhishek was confused but agreed, trusting Ihfaaz's judgment. It wasn't until he received another call from Ihfaaz weeks later, asking for a meeting in Mumbai, that the full weight of the situation became clear.

When they met, Ihfaaz revealed something that shook Abhishek to his core—a bombshell that changed everything he thought he knew.

The plan was in place, and Abhishek's heart pounded as he processed the enormity of what Ihfaaz had laid out before him. Three names—Rizwan Sheikh, Faheem Ali, and Shabir Khan—had been handed to him by his mentor. The men were remnants of a feared past, now reduced to desperate shadows of their former selves. Ihfaaz had found them in Ranchi, where they were hiding, evading arrest for some time, willing to do anything for money.

Ihfaaz's instructions were precise, almost cold in their clarity. "Inflate their egos, Abhishek," he said, "make them believe they're special. Tell them they were recommended for a job only they can handle."

"But what's the job?" Abhishek asked.

"They need to kill me."

"What?" Abhishek stared, stunned. The weight of the words hit him like a punch to the gut.

Ihfaaz held up a hand, signalling for calm. "Listen, you'll provide them with fake guns—movie props. They'll think they're shooting at me, but no real harm will be done. I'll arrange two identical cars: one for the attack, one as a getaway. The second car will have real guns in the trunk and empty shell casings on the floor. You'll make sure some of the bullets are found at the crime scene, and hand over a couple of bullets to the doctor. He will list them as being taken out of my body."

"And the getaway?" Abhishek asked, still grappling with the enormity of the plan.

"They'll switch to the second car after the attack. There will be a phone in the glove box. When you're sure they've reached the outskirts of town, use the phone I give you to call that number which will trigger a neat little blast. That will ensure our 'assassins' disappear before I even reach the hospital."

Abhishek could hardly believe what he was hearing. "Bhai, this is dangerous. There are too many things that could go wrong. Why take such a risk? Why not let me help you without putting your life on the line like this?"

Ihfaaz's eyes hardened. "This is the gamble I must take, Abhishek. You have no idea what's at stake. If I fail, I die. But if I succeed, I'll gain everything I've ever wanted. This is how you repay me—you've always wanted to, haven't you? This is the time."

Abhishek's hesitation was evident. The plan was complex, full of pitfalls. But Ihfaaz's conviction left no room for doubt. Reluctantly, he agreed. Then, as an afterthought, Ihfaaz added, "There's one more thing. On the day of the attack, you need to be in the flat adjacent to my office building—right behind the shooters. You will fire two real bullets at me."

Abhishek's heart froze.

Ihfaaz continued, "I trust you're an expert marksman, right? Make sure you hit where there's minimal damage. I'm putting my life in your hands, Abhishek. Don't mess it up. Or else... well, I'll die for real."

"Bhai," Abhishek whispered, still stunned by the gravity of what he was being asked to do, "what if something goes wrong?"

Ihfaaz smiled. "Just make sure it doesn't."

The day of the attack arrived. Everything went according to plan—almost. The three hired shooters, as instructed, arrived at the scene, their egos inflated, their confidence fuelled by alcohol. They took their positions and fired their blanks, believing they were part of a real hit. But as Ihfaaz stood in front of them, something went awry. One of the shooters noticed a malfunction with his fake gun and, without hesitation, pulled out a country-made pistol. The real bullet grazed Ihfaaz's shoulder, causing more damage than planned.

From the flat behind, Abhishek took a deep breath, aimed carefully, and fired two real bullets into Ihfaaz's body—just as instructed. He hit the targets precisely where he had been told, ensuring minimal damage. But the unexpected shot from the country-made pistol caused more harm than anyone had anticipated.

When Abhishek arrived at the hospital and heard about the additional injury, his heart sank. The wound was worse than expected, leading to extra blood loss and poisoning, prolonging Ihfaaz's stay in the ICU. Frustrated and anxious, Abhishek found himself in a heated argument with Nadia, a conflict that, in an ironic twist, kept her from interacting with him further. She wanted nothing to do with him, and that was a blessing.

For days, Abhishek stationed himself at the hospital, consumed by guilt and fear over Ihfaaz's condition. When he finally received news that Ihfaaz had regained consciousness, he rushed to his side.

"Bhai," Abhishek said, his voice thick with emotion, "I'm sorry. That extra bullet, it wasn't supposed to happen."

Ihfaaz, pale but smiling, waved him off. "It's just a little collateral damage. Small compared to what we've achieved."

Abhishek sighed, still burdened by guilt. But there was no time for dwelling on the past. In a private room, away from prying eyes, Abhishek couldn't help but ask, "Why those three, Bhai? We could have used anyone. Why risk it with them?"

Ihfaaz's eyes darkened for a moment. "Those three crossed me once, Abhishek. Years ago, they took a contract to kill me. This was my chance to settle that score—and they served a higher purpose. But I must tell you, Abhishek Patil, you are one gem of a person, and I'm proud to call you my friend. You truly are your father's son."

With those words, Ihfaaz pulled Abhishek into a weak embrace. As Abhishek left the room, he found himself thinking not just about the dangerous game Ihfaaz was playing, but about how much he still had to learn from—and about—the man people considered as *The Facilitator* and he considered him to be his mentor.

Chapter 38

Despite the hint given to Varda by the constable, she did not travel to Sultanabad immediately. But after a week, when charges of treason against the country and printing of fake currency were added to the list of crimes against Fazil Hussain and his son-in-law, she found it inevitable to make the journey. She arrived at Ihfaaz's office, unaware of his true identity, and requested an appointment. The receptionist took her name and asked her to wait while she checked if Ihfaaz was available.

Nadia, attending the call, froze when she heard the name. *Varda*. Shock coursed through her. "What is this woman doing here?" she muttered under her breath. She put the call on hold and informed Ihfaaz that Varda had come to see him.

Ihfaaz looked at Nadia calmly and said, "Let her in."

Nadia was puzzled by his reaction but said nothing, hiding her own bubbling emotions. Ihfaaz excused himself, saying he needed to freshen up in the washroom, leaving Nadia to greet Varda. When Varda entered the room, she glanced around nervously, noticing the empty main chair. Her eyes briefly met Nadia's, who was seated next to it.

"I wanted to meet Ihfaaz sir," Varda said hesitantly, shifting her weight uncomfortably as she glanced around.

Nadia was silently evaluating her, studying the lines on her face, the weariness in her eyes. Varda looked harried and tired, wrinkles forming around her eyes and forehead, and even a hint of grey in her hair. Despite the passage of time, Nadia could tell that Varda must have once been a beauty—perhaps that's what had captivated Ihfaaz years ago. Now, time and circumstances had worn her down.

No wonder Ihfaaz had fallen for her, Nadia thought bitterly.

Nadia gestured for Varda to sit on the couch and said, "Ihfaaz sir will be here in a few minutes. What brings you here?"

Varda's voice was quiet. "It's personal."

Nadia nodded, maintaining her composure despite the storm raging inside her. The two women sat in tense silence, waiting for Ihfaaz to return. When the door to the washroom finally opened, Varda straightened up on the couch, her breath catching in her throat as Ihfaaz walked into the room, wiping his face with a towel.

As Ihfaaz's face came into view, Varda's eyes widened in shock. She gasped, staring at him in disbelief. This was impossible—either it was a horrifying coincidence, or Ahsan had risen from the dead.

Ihfaaz sat down beside Nadia, facing Varda. His face was different, his voice slightly changed, but the aura was unmistakably the same. "You wanted to meet me?" he asked, his voice measured, though a flicker of something dark simmered beneath the surface.

Varda couldn't speak for a moment, her mind reeling. This wasn't just a meeting with a stranger—it was Ahsan. Her past, her darkest sins, had come crashing back into her life.

"My father, my brothers, and my husband... they've all been arrested," Varda stammered, struggling to find her voice. "They're facing countless charges, and every day new ones are added. They're being told to confess to attempting to kill you, and I was told that only you can help us. Please... help us. We didn't do anything."

Ihfaaz's expression didn't change. He remained silent for a moment, letting her words hang in the air before responding coldly. "So, you're Fazil Hussain's daughter," he said. "The one who sent three men to have me killed."

"No!" Varda cried, her voice shaking. "My father didn't do that. I swear, we had nothing to do with this."

"Come on, Varda," Ihfaaz's voice grew icier. "Who are you trying to fool? Don't you remember? Fifteen years ago, your father handed over the contract to kill me when I was hiding in Kolkata, trying to avoid arrest. That was after *you* had put false accusations on me."

Varda's eyes grew wider, and her lips trembled. "Ahsan...," she whispered, barely able to form the name.

"Yes, Varda," Ihfaaz replied, his voice laced with venom. "Ahsan. The man you betrayed. The man whose life you ruined. I didn't force you to marry me. You had a choice, but instead, you destroyed me, destroyed my family. While we were celebrating our engagement, you were plotting to tear my world apart."

Tears welled up in Varda's eyes. "I'm sorry," she whispered, her voice broken. "I'm so sorry, Ahsan."

Ihfaaz's voice rose, filled with the weight of years of pent-up rage. "Sorry? You think that's enough? Do you think an apology will erase the fifteen years my mother spent mourning my death? Will it undo the life I could've had? I had a family, Varda—parents, siblings—but I had to leave them, to exile myself, just to protect them. Do you know the real pain of exile, Varda? It's not living in a foreign land. It's being forced to live away from the people you love, while they live under the shadow of your sins."

Varda sobbed harder now, collapsing under the weight of his words. "I know I've sinned, Ahsan," she choked out. "I've paid for it. The Almighty has punished me—I can't have children. I've been cursed to live a life of loneliness and taunts from my in-laws. I know it's not enough, but I've been suffering, too. Please... forgive me. Forgive my family. Please help us."

With that, Varda collapsed to the floor, clutching at Ihfaaz's feet in desperation. Nadia sat in silence, watching the scene unfold. She felt a strange mix of pity and anger for Varda, but most of all, her heart ached for Ihfaaz. She finally understood the depths of his pain, the years of torment he had endured.

Ihfaaz looked down at Varda, his expression unmoved. He had spent years suffering in silence, and now, this broken woman before him wanted forgiveness.

Ihfaaz stood up, towering over Varda, his presence intimidating, his voice cutting through the tension like ice. "There is no forgiveness, Varda. You destroyed everything I once was, and now you will live in the ruins of your own making. Go back to that hollow life, barren and cursed, just as you made mine. Let every breath remind you that this is the fate you chose. And remember," he leaned closer, his eyes burning with hatred, "no matter how much you beg, no matter where you turn, there will never be mercy for you—not in this life, or the next."

Varda's eyes widened with the weight of his words. Her breath hitched as she realized that her desperate pleas had fallen on deaf ears. The world around her seemed to collapse as she struggled to stand.

Finally, Nadia, who had been silently watching the encounter unfold, stepped forward. Without a word, she gently but firmly took Varda's arm and guided her out of the office. Varda stumbled, her spirit broken, as the door closed behind them.

Nadia returned to the office and found Ihfaaz sitting in his chair, his eyes closed, lost in thought. She approached him carefully, tapped his shoulder lightly, and whispered, "Ihfaaz?"

Without opening his eyes, he responded in a quiet, weary voice, "Nadia, can you please give me some time alone?"

Sensing the heaviness in his words, Nadia nodded silently and left, closing the door gently behind her. Ihfaaz sat there, still, the weight of the confrontation with Varda hanging over him like a dark cloud. He had spent years building his life around revenge, and now, having achieved it, he felt an unexpected hollowness. The rage that had fuelled him for so long had burned out, leaving only an unsettling emptiness in its place. He had finally achieved everything he set out to do, but instead of victory, it felt like a loss—a loss of purpose, of direction.

After a while, Ihfaaz stood up, his mind still swirling with unresolved thoughts. Without saying a word, he left his office and went home, seeking solitude.

Later, Nadia returned to the office, expecting to check in on Ihfaaz. When she realized he wasn't there, her heart sank. She stepped out into the hallway and approached one of the staff members.

"Ihfaaz sir has left for home," the man informed her. "He said he'll get in touch with you tomorrow morning. He specifically asked not to be disturbed for the rest of the day."

Nadia nodded, her concern deepening. She understood that something had shifted within Ihfaaz, something deeper than just the confrontation with Varda. But for now, all she could do was wait.

The N.E.S.T. story

The conference hall of N.E.S.T. headquarters buzzed with anticipation as Arun Singh entered, commanding immediate attention from the assembled members - the governing committee, the heads of various departments and some veterans of the agency. This rare gathering of the governing committee was a testament to the significance of the day's announcements. As the room fell silent, Arun Singh began his speech, the gravity of his words sinking in with each sentence.

Arun Singh, with a voice tinged with both resolve and nostalgia, announced his retirement from N.E.S.T. He revealed that despite his colleagues' insistence on his departure, the toll of his demanding work on his health had made it imperative for him to step down. The decision was bittersweet, but it was clear that the time had come for a new leader to guide the organization.

The room, filled with the highest echelons of N.E.S.T., listened attentively as Arun Singh continued. The first major change he introduced was the appointment of Shalini Rao as the new Deputy Director of Operations. Shalini's rise to this prestigious position marked a historic moment, as she became the first female to hold this role. Her transition from heading counterintelligence to this new role was met with enthusiastic applause from her colleagues.

Next, Arun Singh announced Vikram Naidu's promotion to head counterintelligence, a role previously held by Shalini. The final revelation was that Colonel Aditya Malhotra, currently Deputy Director of Operations, would be taking over as the new Director. The news was met with a mixture of excitement and nostalgia as the attendees recognized the end of an era with Arun Singh's departure.

Following the formal announcements, the atmosphere in the hall was one of celebration and admiration. Shalini, Vikram, and Aditya were congratulated warmly by their peers, and everyone expressed their deep respect for Arun Singh's contributions to N.E.S.T. The sense of loss at his departure was palpable, and many felt the weight of his absence.

In the quieter moments that followed, Arun Singh took Aditya aside to discuss the transition. He outlined that for the next two months, Aditya would work closely with him to ensure a smooth handover and better understand the intricacies of the role.

Their conversation soon shifted to Ihfaaz, whose collaboration with N.E.S.T. had proven to be extraordinarily beneficial. Arun Singh shared the details of their partnership with Aditya, highlighting the significant advantages it had brought to the agency. Ihfaaz's provision of critical information had enabled N.E.S.T. to identify key players involved in transferring money for espionage activities. The details of money trails and ATM card usage had been instrumental in uncovering sleeper cells across the country.

Aditya, intrigued and somewhat wary, asked how best to handle Ihfaaz. Arun Singh offered a word of caution, advising Aditya to continue using Vikram as the intermediary between Ihfaaz and N.E.S.T. He also warned Aditya of Ihfaaz's shrewdness and intelligence, recounting how Ihfaaz had managed to outfox him in the past in Kolkata. Arun Singh felt that it seemed that Ihfaaz manipulated some or all events in Sultanabad to make it appear as though he was doing N.E.S.T. a favour, when in fact, it was the agency that did him a favour. But he could not pin point towards any concrete fact to back his intuition.

Arun Singh concluded with a note of caution: Ihfaaz was a prized asset, but handling him required careful consideration. Aditya was advised to maintain the façade of mutual benefit while remaining vigilant of Ihfaaz's potential to outsmart them.

Chapter 39

The next morning, Nadia woke up later than usual. It had been a restless night, her mind buzzing with everything that had transpired the previous day. She had barely slept, her thoughts going back and forth, unsure of what to make of Ihfaaz's sudden behaviour. The weight of his cold words to Varda still lingered in her mind. Yet, she had felt relieved when he left, trusting that he needed space.

As she shuffled into the kitchen, she quickly fixed herself a simple breakfast—just a slice of toast and coffee, not feeling up for much more. It was a quiet morning, one of those rare days when the city outside seemed calm. Nadia rarely received visitors, especially unannounced, so she nearly jumped when the doorbell rang. She paused for a moment, wondering who it could be. After all, it wasn't normal for anyone to show up at this hour.

Curiosity getting the better of her, Nadia walked over to the door and peered through the peephole. To her shock, she found Ihfaaz standing outside, looking far different than she had ever seen him before. He was dressed in his best clothes, immaculately put together, holding a bouquet of roses in his hand. She froze for a moment, her brain struggling to catch up with her eyes. **What was he doing here?** And why dressed like that?

Hurriedly, she unlocked the door and opened it wide, still staring at him in stunned silence. "Ihfaaz?" she managed to whisper, her voice barely audible.

He gave her a soft smile, breaking through her shock. "May I come in?" he asked politely, as if they were strangers, and not two people who had known each other for over a decade.

Nadia snapped out of her daze, suddenly embarrassed. "Oh! Yes, yes, please, come in." She stepped aside, still flustered, her heart racing for reasons she couldn't yet understand. She was still wearing her oldest, most worn-out clothes—faded track pants and an oversized t-shirt—and couldn't help but feel self-conscious next to his formal appearance.

"You can join me for breakfast," she offered awkwardly, still trying to make sense of what was happening. "I just made some coffee."

But Ihfaaz shook his head gently. "No, thank you. I already had my breakfast. But I won't mind a cup of coffee."

He handed her the bouquet of roses, his expression calm, almost serene. Nadia, still a little dazed, took them and stared down at the flowers in her hand, wondering what in the world was going on. She quickly placed them on the dining table and gestured for him to sit down, which he did.

As she poured coffee for him, she noticed the unusual silence between them. The air was thick with tension, but not the kind she was used to. This was different. It was as if Ihfaaz had come with a purpose, but she couldn't put her finger on what it was. He had been distant the day before, withdrawn after his encounter with Varda, and now here he was, showing up unannounced, dressed like this, with flowers no less.

Finally, after what felt like an eternity, Ihfaaz spoke, breaking the silence. "Nadia," he began, his voice low but steady. "You've known me for more than 10 years now."

She felt her heart sink. His tone was serious, too serious. Was something wrong? Was this leading to something bad?

"You're the only person who knows about my past and my present," he continued. "I've always appreciated everything you've done for me."

Nadia's heart pounded. **What was he trying to say?** It felt like he was preparing her for something terrible, and she braced herself for whatever was coming next. Her mind raced, jumping to conclusions. Was he leaving? Was he pushing her away after all they'd been through? His words sounded like a goodbye, and the very thought of that crushed her.

But then Ihfaaz continued, his eyes never leaving hers. "I don't want to keep you in the dark. You know what I've been through. The kind of work I do... it requires secrecy, even from those closest to me. I don't want any complications after marriage."

The word **marriage** hit her like a bolt of lightning.

She blinked, staring at him in disbelief, barely able to register what he had just said.

He went on, his voice softer now. "That is... if you still want to marry me."

Nadia was completely caught off guard. **Marry him?** He was proposing? After all these years, after everything they had been through, after all the unspoken emotions between them, here he was, sitting at her dining table, casually asking her to marry him—while she sat there in her old, faded clothes, with half a piece of toast still on her plate. She hadn't expected this. Not today. Not like this.

She blinked again, trying to form words, but none came out. Instead, without thinking, she dropped the piece of toast in her hand and practically launched herself at him. Wrapping her arms around him, she hugged him tightly, burying her face in his chest.

"Yes!" she cried, her voice trembling with emotion. "Oh my God, yes! Of course, I'll marry you, Ihfaaz!"

Tears welled up in her eyes as she clung to him, feeling years of unspoken love, years of silent support, and waiting finally give way to something real. She had loved him for so long, but she had never imagined this moment would come—not like this, not now, but she was more than ready.

She pulled back just enough to look up at him, her eyes filled with tears of joy. "I've been waiting for this for so long," she whispered, her voice breaking. "I don't care about the past, or the secrets, or anything else. I've always known who you are, Ihfaaz, and that's all that matters. We'll face whatever comes together. I just want to be with you."

In that moment, as she looked into his eyes, she could see something shift in him. The weight of the past, the burden of his secrets, seemed to lighten, even if just for a moment. He placed a gentle hand on her cheek, his thumb brushing away the tear that had fallen. For the first time in what felt like forever, there was peace between them—an unspoken understanding that they were finally stepping into a new chapter, together.

This wasn't just a proposal. It was the beginning of something they had both been yearning for, something they had both silently hoped for but never voiced. And now, here it was, laid bare between them.

Epilogue

Ihfaaz was nestled comfortably in the drawing room of his new bungalow, playing with his twins—a boy and a girl. It was a rare Sunday off from work, and he savoured the moment of family togetherness. Nadia, busy preparing breakfast, had managed to make this Sunday special. After their whirlwind marriage and the grand reception, life had settled into a joyous routine.

The quick turnaround from their engagement to marriage had been both unexpected and heartwarming. Ihfaaz had informed his parents of his decision to marry Nadia, and they were overjoyed. While they had initially suggested a wedding in Kushalgram, Ihfaaz chose to host the ceremony in Sultanabad, bringing the family together for a celebration that bridged both worlds. Before the wedding he travelled to Kushalgram to meet his entire family. The reunion was emotional, filled with apologies and forgiveness, and it strengthened the bonds within his family.

The wedding was a grand affair, with Faraz Khan's entire family in attendance, marking a dream come true for Nadia. She had seamlessly blended into the family, and the marriage was a resounding success.

In the months following their marriage, Ihfaaz and Nadia had moved into a beautiful bungalow with a spacious lawn. Life had been blissful. Professionally, Ihfaaz had seen tremendous success. The once shell companies had transformed into thriving legitimate enterprises, while the hawala business was efficiently managed by Pradip and his team.

Dinu Kaka, a revered figure passed away a month after Ihfaaz's marriage. His death was a significant loss, but he left behind a legacy of success. D.P. Logistics and Courier had become one of the top five courier and logistics companies under his stewardship of his son Samir.

The company was so successful that Samir had taken it public, listing it on the stock market. The market cap had soared to 4000 crores, and Ihfaaz's 5% stake in the company was worth a substantial 200 crores.

Fazil Hussain, his sons, and son-in-law were still imprisoned. Though Nadia had persuaded Ihfaaz to drop some charges and show leniency, the genuine charges ensured they would spend the next 20 to 25 years in prison. Out of compassion for Varda, and with Ihfaaz's reluctant consent, Nadia had arranged a monthly allowance for Varda and her mother to ease their financial burden. Varda had accepted this as her new reality.

As Ihfaaz enjoyed a peaceful morning with his family, his phone buzzed with a call from Vikram. Vikram was outside the bungalow and wished to meet Ihfaaz. Ihfaaz instructed the security guard to let Vikram in. He sent the kids inside and welcomed Vikram into his home.

After the customary pleasantries, Vikram informed Ihfaaz that the agency had offered Abhishek a position in the agency. Ihfaaz feigned surprise, though he was already aware of the development, in fact Abhishek had already given his consent to join the agency. He knew that Vikram's visit had a deeper purpose.

Vikram, with a touch of hesitation, asked Ihfaaz for a personal favour. His daughter wished to join A.K.P.N. College, Mumbai, but despite their efforts, they were unable to secure a seat. Ihfaaz assured Vikram he would do everything in his power to facilitate the admission.

He made a few quick calls, and within ten minutes, he returned with good news. The admission was secured, and they don't need to pay any fees. Consider this as a gift from Ihfaaz to Vikram's daughter. Vikram was overwhelmed by the swift resolution and began to express his gratitude. Just then, Nadia, unaware of Vikram's presence, called out to Ihfaaz.

"Ihfaaz ji, if you wish to have breakfast today morning itself, then can you please watch your kids? They are not letting me cook."

With a smile, Ihfaaz turned to Vikram. "That's Mrs. calling. Over the past three years, I've learned that whenever she calls me Ihfaaz ji, I'm in trouble. Please wait here; I'll go pacify the Mrs. and handle the kids."

As Ihfaaz went to attend to his family, Vikram sat in the drawing room, marvelling at Ihfaaz's ability to resolve what he had struggled with for a month. It was clear why Ihfaaz was known as "***The Facilitator***."

www.ingramcontent.com/pod-product-compliance
Lightning Source LLC
LaVergne TN
LVHW041200150826
845673LV00001B/239
* 9 7 9 8 8 9 5 5 6 9 6 6 5 *